HAWKE'S HONOR

THE AEGIS NETWORK: JACKSONVILLE DIVISION

JEN TALTY

JUPITER PRESS

PRAISE FOR JEN TALTY

"Deadly Secrets is the best of romance and suspense in one hot read!" *NYT Bestselling Author Jennifer Probst*

"A charming setting and a steamy couple heat up the pages in a suspenseful story I couldn't put down!" *NY Times and USA today Bestselling Author Donna Grant*

"Jen Talty's books will grab your attention and pull you into a world of relatable characters, strong personalities, humor, and believable storylines. You'll laugh, you'll cry, and you'll rush to get the next book she releases!" Natalie Ann USA Today Bestselling Author

"I positively loved *In Two Weeks*, and highly recommend it. The writing is wonderful, the story is fantastic, and the characters will keep you coming back for more. I can't wait to get my hands on future installments of the NYS Troopers series." *Long and Short Reviews*

"*In Two Weeks* hooks the reader from page one. This is a fast paced story where the development of the romance grabs you emotionally and the suspense keeps you sitting on the edge of your chair. Great characters, great writing, and a believable plot that can be a warning to all of us." *Desiree Holt, USA Today Bestseller*

"*Dark Water* delivers an engaging portrait of wounded hearts as the memorable characters take you on a healing journey of love. A mysterious death brings danger and intrigue into the drama, while sultry passions brew into a believable plot that melts the reader's heart. Jen Talty pens an entertaining romance that grips the heart as the colorful and dangerous story unfolds into a chilling ending." *Night Owl Reviews*

"This is not the typical love story, nor is it the typical mystery. The characters are well rounded and interesting." *You Gotta Read Reviews*

"Murder in Paradise Bay is a fast-paced romantic thriller with plenty of twists and turns to keep you guessing until the end. You won't want to miss this one..." *USA Today bestselling author Janice Maynard*

Hawke Wilson walked away from the love of his life after a devastating tragedy, choosing to never look back. He ignored every letter his ex-girlfriend sent, burying them—and his past—in a box while throwing himself into his work as a paramedic, firefighter, and Aegis Network operative. But when a 9-1-1 call turns into a nightmare, Hawke is forced to relive the worst day of his life. His world is shaken when he comes face-to-face with Calista Alba once more, but nothing could have prepared him for the revelation of his ten-year-old son.

Calista never intended to keep Hawke's son from him, but when he left the Air Force and disappeared without a trace, she had no choice but to move forward. Still, she did everything she could to keep the memory of Hawke alive for herself and for their son. Now that fate has brought them together again, Hawke is determined to make things right. But when a dangerous investigation puts Calista and their child in the crosshairs, Hawke will stop at nothing to protect the family he never knew he had —and fight for a second chance.

NOTE FROM THE AUTHOR

Hello everyone!

It is important to note that this book was originally titled *Remember Me Always* and written as part of the Susan Stoker *Special Forces: Operation Alpha* world. Since the rights to the book have reverted back to me, I have stripped the story of all the elements from Susan's world (as it was legally required of me to do so) as well as changing the names of some of my characters so it would fit nicely into my Aegis Network series.

I have also expanded the story, adding scenes and updating a few things. I'm much happier with the storyline and characters now. I've always loved this series, but as with many things that I wrote years ago, I felt as though I could have done better.

Please enjoy!
Jen Talty

For my husband. You are my rock. My center. Thank you for being there when I needed you most.

PROLOGUE

TEN YEARS AGO...

"*H*ave you heard from her?"

Hawke Wilson tossed his cell phone on the bed. He'd read the email his ex-girlfriend had sent him a dozen times. Each time he read the words, he prayed that she was doing exactly what she'd done every single time. She felt he'd completely and utterly turned his back on her. That this would be exactly like every other time, and she'd been seeking attention.

His attention.

But something tickled the back of his brain that, this time, she'd gone and done it.

"No," Calista Alba, his current girlfriend, said.

His chest tightened. He couldn't believe after all these years, he was still dealing with this shit.

Everyone told him he was nuts for even being friends with Courtney. Hell, he'd broken up with Courtney more than once based on these types of antics. Her high drama and need to be at the center of his world had become too much to handle.

And not just for him.

Everyone around her had grown tired of her constant games, manipulations, and going dark for hours, even days sometimes, making everyone worry she'd gone and hurt herself, when in reality, she only wanted people to suffer as she believed she had.

However, something felt very different this time. So much had changed. It had been five years since they'd graduated from college. He'd continued with his career in the Air Force. He was living his dream, and Courtney was no longer a part of his future.

No matter how hard he tried to clarify that, she couldn't accept it.

"Why don't you try texting her?" he asked Calista, who happened to be Courtney's ex-best friend. They had gone through their own friendship breakup and it hadn't been pretty. He was partly to blame for that too.

"Trust me, I have." Calista paced in a circle in her tiny one-bedroom apartment as she gnawed on her nails. Their relationship had been strained over the last two years in part by his constant deployments, which there was nothing he could do about. Calista supported his career and never made it difficult for him to leave. She always kissed him goodbye, whispering in his ear to be careful and to have his buddies' six. Calista was good about things like that. But while he was gone, Courtney would always do her best to wedge herself into their relationship, trying to put crazy ideas in Calista's head.

It always came back to Courtney. She had followed him to his first base after he'd graduated from the Air Force Academy. He'd told her not to come. That he needed time and space. He wasn't sure he could continue being in a relationship with her, not only because of her jealous rampages but because of her constant threats. But she moved anyway. The hardest part had been Calista. She had gone to Delaware State University for her undergraduate degree and was continuing on for her doctorate. When he'd first moved there, he'd been excited to have someone from home to talk to. Someone who understood what he'd been going through.

He'd leaned on Calista.

And then he fell in love with her.

3

She was the one he wanted to marry and have children with.

Life could sometimes be unfair. He'd never wanted to hurt Courtney, but that's exactly what he'd done.

And in the worst of ways.

"I've called her parents and everyone else I can think of. No one has heard from her since last night."

"You called her parents?" Hawke's voice rose an octave higher than usual. "Why worry them until we know more?"

"Are you kidding?" Calista raised her palms toward the ceiling. She'd always been a strong, independent woman. With her upbringing, she'd been forced to grow up too fast. Some people thought her life experiences had hardened her, making her cold and detached.

Hawke knew that wasn't true. Calista had a heart of gold filled with compassion and empathy for those who suffered, especially those with mental illness. She understood Courtney better than anyone. Calista had told Hawke a hundred times that Courtney was never going to stop until he stopped enabling her and allowing her to keep her unhealthy attachment to him alive.

It had put a distance between them and he resented both Calista and Courtney for it.

Calista had made it very clear to Courtney that while she loved her like a sister and wanted the best for her, she wouldn't continue to put up with games. Either they were best friends or they weren't.

Courtney told Calista to break up with him, and then they could go back to the way things were. Hawke had thought that might be a good idea, but then he'd lose the one thing he loved more than life itself. Calista refused to be held emotionally hostage to anyone, even her best friend.

"Besides the fact that Courtney could have been with her parents all this time, they have the right to know." Calista shook her head. "And I told them about the email."

Hawke opened his mouth but snapped it shut quickly when Calista shot her hand up a few inches from his face. "Courtney has a mental illness. She needs professional help. I'm a licensed therapist, but I can't be the one to help her. I'm too close. I'm also part of the problem in her eyes. I've begged her to see a counselor. I've given her a dozen recommendations. She won't do it."

"All we've done is hurt her," he said with a

sarcastic tone that matched his fake smile. "She lost both of us."

Calista narrowed her stare, bringing her big, beautiful aqua eyes into tiny snakelike slits. "I'm so tired of arguing with you whenever she does this. You broke up with her a long time before we ever got together. You put your feelings for me on hold because you wanted to give her time to get over you and I love you for that. It's not our fault that Courtney is unbalanced." A couple of quick tears dribbled down Calista's face. She swiped at them with her fingers. "I tried to help her get over you. Help her move on. I spent hours trying to convince her that it wasn't the breakup or even you. That it's anything and everything that sets her off. You didn't end our friendship. It died when I broke her confidence and went to her parents with my concerns about her mental well-being. Not when we got together."

Hawke pinched the bridge of his nose. "This is different. It's worse than when she learned about us. Her hearing that we're talking about moving in together was a lot."

"But it's our lives and it's not fair that it's being dictated by her." Calista let out a long breath. "We both know she would have gone batshit over any girl you went out with. It was just one more thing she could use to keep herself living in the delusions she created. And we don't know if she's done anything to herself. Hawke, she pulls this shit all the time whenever something in your life changes, and you fall for it hook, line, and sinker. It's got to stop."

Hawke dropped his arms to his sides, trying to keep his heart from racing in panic. He leaned against the counter and rubbed his temples. At one time, Courtney seemed like the most put-together person he'd ever known and way out of his league, even though he'd known her his entire life. It had always shocked him that she agreed to go to the senior ball with him, marking their first official date. That entire summer had been one of the best summers on record. But then he went off to the Air Force Academy and things shifted. Her letters got weird. And he couldn't come home that first summer and it drove her crazy. She'd become wildly possessive and insanely jealous. He needed to focus on his education and what would become his career.

They broke up.

And got back together.

And that cycle repeated until he was twenty-three years old.

He was twenty-eight and for the last four years, he'd been with Calista. The first year things were great, but they lived their relationship in secret. The second year had been hell. But the next year things had settled down a bit. He believed Courtney had finally moved on, but eight months ago, it had all started again.

"I know that," he said softly. Initially, he thought it all had to do with Courtney's parents getting a divorce. He still figured that had been the catalyst. But she'd changed. She wasn't the same bubbly person he'd fallen hard for.

She'd been his first love, and he knew there would always be a special place in his heart for her, but he didn't love her.

He loved Calista.

He ran a hand over his face as he sucked in a gulp of air. Guilt tore through his gut. Courtney cried wolf a million times since he'd gone off and fallen in love with Calista. She would show up at the base and wait at the gate. She would bang on Calista's door, when she knew he'd spent the night, which was most evenings when he was in town. He'd get phone calls, text messages, and emails, all with her threatening to kill herself.

Before he started dating Calista, he did what he

thought was right, and he'd go back to her, hoping that he'd be able to show her just how bad they'd become for each other.

Lifting his gaze, he stared at Calista. She'd swooped in and stolen his heart. He knew if he lost her, it would crush him, so he understood a little about how Courtney might have felt.

"I know what you're thinking," Calista said as tears ran down her cheeks, taking a small trail of mascara with them.

He nodded.

"I know. We should have been the ones to tell her about us, and it's frustrating that she learned about us possibly moving in together, but what is done is done." Calista closed the gap. She rested her hands on his chest. Her long dark hair flowed over her shoulders, and her bright-blue eyes had captivated him for months before he'd even allowed himself to ask her out.

She'd been Courtney's best friend since grade school, and he was the asshole who ruined their friendship.

"It was going to come out sometime, and we can't constantly be responsible for Courtney's well-being. She's been holding both of us hostage for almost ten years," Calista said.

Hawke didn't know exactly when he'd fallen for Calista. It was weird because he'd known her since middle school but hadn't ever noticed her in that way. One day, after one of Courtney's many attempts to force Hawke into taking her back, he'd gone to Calista and that was it.

Courtney had often pulled the same kind of stunts with her best friend. If Calista did anything with her other friends and Courtney was omitted, Courtney would drum up some drama, making Calista feel bad, forcing her to cancel her plans. But she stopped doing that at the end of high school. She even went to a different college, changing their lifelong plan of being roommates. Calista told Hawke he should do the same. Something about a little tough love might be enough to give her the wake-up call she needed.

"The last time we ignored her, she attempted to kill herself." Hawke took Calista's hands, kissed her palms, and then pushed her away. He knew deep down he had no reason to feel guilty. He and Courtney had been done for a year before anything had happened with Calista, but the second Courtney found out, she went nuts by taking a sledgehammer to his pickup and then writing *cheater* all over it in spray paint.

That had been fun to drive onto the base.

She also slit Calista's tires and spray-painted her car with *slut, whore, bitch*.

"No, she didn't," Calista said. "If she'd been taken to the hospital, as she claimed, they would have held her in the psych ward. It's standard procedure." She cocked a brow. "I do this shit for a living. And she was out of the hospital in less than three hours. She didn't try. She only said that to make you feel better."

"I hate it when you sound like a fucking therapist." Hawke knew Calista was right. On all counts, but he couldn't shake the guilt.

Or the bad feeling in the pit of his gut.

Calista laughed. "Don't be a dick and toss my career in my face. I don't do that to you." She reached across the counter and snagged her clutch purse. "I need to run to the store. You're welcome to stay or leave. Whatever suits your fancy."

The sound of an old-fashioned telephone rang out, filling the room with tension so thick it was palpable.

Hawke lunged for his cell. "It's Courtney's mom." He swallowed the thick lump of bile that crept into his throat. He quickly tapped to accept the call, hit the speaker button, and coughed. "Hello? Mrs. Baker?"

The sound of sniffling echoed in the kitchen. His heartbeat burst in his head. He gripped the counter for support.

"They found her," Mrs. Baker said. "She hung herself at the school playground."

One week later...

Calista leaned against the tree in the cemetery, her eyes dry and itchy from days of crying. The sun beat on her face, making her hairline bead in perspiration, reminding her that she was alive, and her former best friend was not.

The therapist knew this was not her fault, even though Courtney had all but blamed Calista and her relationship with Hawke as one of the many reasons she killed herself, something that Calista would have to live with for the rest of her life.

Only a few people milled about the dreary cemetery as a long line of cars followed the dark limo toward the exit.

Hawke stood before the casket, decked out in his Air Force uniform. He looked so dashing in that damn thing. They hadn't moved in together yet because he'd been contemplating his next career move. If he stayed in the Air Force, he'd be transferred to a new base, and she'd already decided she'd go with him. If he left, she'd go wherever he went as well. She loved him. He was her person.

But the other reason had been Courtney. As long as they lived in the same city, he didn't want to throw their relationship in her face, and Calista could honestly accept that.

He stuffed his hands in his pockets, and his head bowed.

She pushed from the tree and headed toward Courtney's resting place. "Hey, you," Calista said, slipping her hand under his arm.

His muscles tensed and twitched as if she poked him with a fire stick. "What are you still doing here?" He jerked away.

A sharp pain like a knife stabbing her in the chest caught hold in her gut. "Waiting for you. We haven't talked in a few days, and I've worried about you." She started feeling stalkerish as she left him one text and voice message after the other. She knew he had to have gotten them; the only question was, why had he shut her out completely?

"I'm fine," he said. "I was going to call you later. We need to talk."

"Okay." She reached for his hand, but once again, he pulled away. She dug her heel into the grass. "What's going on? Why are you pushing me away? I love you, and I'm hurting too."

He took one step back and folded his arms over his chest. "I've made a decision. I'm following Arthur and the rest of the team. I'm leaving the Air Force. I've got six months left on my contract, and I'll either be deployed or in the field, training."

"Wait, what? You made all those decisions without even discussing them with me?" She dropped her purse to the ground. Her ankles wobbled in her high heels.

Hawke's sarcastic laugh made the hair on her neck stand up. His usually relaxed facial expressions turned to stone. The man glaring at her was not the same man she'd fallen in love with.

"I knew all this was possible, but we said we'd sit down and discuss what was best for us. I told you I'd move wherever you went. Air Force or not. But I can't just do it in a snap of my fingers."

"I'm not asking you to," he said.

The knife turned and twisted, ripping her entire soul apart. "But… but… what about all our plans? Our future."

"Our future died with Courtney." He pointed to the gravesite.

"Now you're talking crazy." The mist falling from the skies rubbed against her eyes like sandpaper.

"Do you want to know what's really crazy?" He pointed his finger between them, back and forth, shaking his head. "This. Us. And the fact you still think there could be an us after reading Courtney's suicide note."

"We didn't kill her," she said behind a clenched jaw. "No one here blames us. What Courtney said in that note was meant to hurt us. To continue to hold us hostage in her death. I've seen it before."

"What she wrote was true. And I blame us. Besides, I can't look at you and not think about her lifeless body hanging in the playground where kids are supposed to run free and laugh without a care in the world." He pounded his chest. "If you had let me take her call then—"

"Right. Maybe she would still be alive, but then she'd go and do it another day. As long as you kept running to her side, she would do that to you.

Guilting you into taking care of her or taking her back. But you know damn well we couldn't fix her." Calista couldn't believe they were having the same argument. She blinked.

"Remind me not to recommend you to my friends, because isn't that what you're supposed to do? Fix people? Not break them?"

Quickly, she took two steps forward and raised her hand, striking his cheek with her palm in a loud smack. Her skin stung, and his face immediately turned bright red. "That was uncalled for."

"My brother will pick up the things I have at your place," he continued in a monotone voice. "I found someone to sublease my apartment for the next couple of months. I'll stay on the base."

"Just like that. We're over." She shook out her hand, unsure if she should slap him again or shake him until he came to his senses.

"Yeah." He nodded. "I'd appreciate it if you didn't call or try to reach me for any reason. I need to move on and like you say, I can't do that if I've got one foot in the past and that's what you are. My past."

"Wow. You're fucking unbelievable. All our hopes and dreams buried with your ex-girlfriend? That's how it's going to be?"

16

"Please don't make this harder than it has to be."

She covered her mouth, hoping to stifle the guttural sob exploding in her belly. "You can't be serious," she managed with a croak.

"Standing here, looking at you, only reminds me that Courtney killed herself, and whether we like it or not, we both played a role in her suicide."

"Hawke, don't—"

"It's done." He glanced over his shoulder. "I already turned in the paperwork to leave the Air Force. Take care, Calista." He turned on his heel and marched off as if she hadn't meant anything to him at all.

"Hawke. Wait!" she cried, but he didn't even pause. If anything, he picked up his pace. "How will I get ahold of you?"

"You won't." He raised his hand over his head and waved, still not turning. "I'm dead to you."

1

Firefighter and paramedic Hawke Wilson rarely took a day off. He worked with the Aegis Network if he wasn't on duty at the fire station. He never once regretted leaving the Air Force. He still got to fight fires and work as a paramedic. Helping people was all he'd ever wanted to do. And he still worked with the best team imaginable. The first year or two after he'd left had been rough, but only because his mind constantly drifted to the past.

Something that still happened. Every damn day. He couldn't rid himself of it, and he tried. For years, he buried himself in women who meant nothing to him in hopes of forgetting both the one he loved.

And the one he destroyed.

But all that did was remind him he was an asshole.

So, he shifted gears and focused on work. That's all he did. All he cared about. His career and the men and women on his team. However, that dynamic had changed a lot over the last ten years.

His brother, Colt, while insanely proud of him, had always been a little disappointed he hadn't joined the Army and Delta Force where they could work side by side. The thought had been appealing, especially when he'd go visit and hang out with Colt's friends.

What a motley crew they were.

Hawke especially enjoyed Clark and Mike, but Peter had a special place in Hawke's heart, having grown up down the street from him. Hawke especially liked his tattoo, which said:

I will honor my brothers-in-arms.

Freedom isn't free and I will defend it with my life.

It is the quiet professional that rules the day.

Colt and Peter were six years older than Hawke. He'd looked up to the two of them his entire life and ended up having these words tattooed across his back:

I will honor my brothers-in-arms along with their loved ones.

Freedom isn't free and I will defend it with my life.

It is the quiet professional that rules the day.

He stood in front of the microwave at the station house, only a few miles from his home near the beach. It had been a busy day of calls. Today, as on most days, he worked as a paramedic, so he only went out when the ambulance did, and today, it had gone out five times. He checked the blinking digital clock flashing before him while his dinner heated.

Five thirty.

He wouldn't be off until seven in the morning. Not that he had anything he needed to do.

"What are you going to do during our vacation? There's going to be a big party on Rex's boat to kick things off," Duncan said.

"I don't plan on attending," Hawke said, wincing. He and Duncan went way back. At one time, they were glued together at the hip. They'd go out on a Friday night, drink, shoot a little pool, and Duncan would enjoy watching Hawke try to pick up women.

Or better yet, they'd both hang back and watch Garth act like a big goof around the ladies.

But all that had changed, like so many other things.

"Too many kids and not enough single women?" Duncan asked with an arched brow. "It's got to be weird being the only single guy left on the crew."

Hawke laughed. Technically, he'd been single for the last ten years. Any woman he'd taken out during that time never lasted more than a month or two. He no longer had the patience or the tolerance to deal with a relationship. "There won't be any single women on that boat, and I'm certainly not looking. Not worth the trouble. I adore all of your kids and could hang with them all day, so that's not the issue."

Damn his captain, Arthur. Or maybe his lieutenant, Rex. It didn't matter. But to require him to take a week off work had been the kiss of death. They even had the nerve to call Timothy at the Aegis Network, informing him of their decision to force Hawke into a so-called much-needed break. Otherwise, he would be spending this week working any and every mission the Aegis Network could throw at him instead of twiddling his thumbs.

Seven days of doing nothing might be some people's idea of heaven.

For Hawke, it only gave him time to think and contemplate his life decisions, and it was during those idle times that *she* would creep into his waking thoughts. It was hard enough that she haunted his dreams on a nightly basis. He had thought the more time and space between them, the more he'd be able to forget.

But he never could.

Just like he could never forgive himself for what happened in the past.

"Then why aren't you coming?" Duncan asked. "This is starting to become a habit with you, and I have to say that Chastity and I are starting to take it personally."

"No offense, but I'm just not in the mood to hang around a bunch of married people and all the stuff that comes with it while trapped on a yacht," Hawke answered honestly.

"That's why I'll be fishing during the day and barhopping at night. Care to join me?" Zach asked, joining him in the kitchen. Zach was a new recruit and a swing on their team when someone was on vacation. Today, it was Buddy, who had to head home to take his wife to a doctor's appointment.

Zach was a good firefighter and a nice kid. Emphasis on *kid*.

"I might just do that," Hawke said.

"I'll text you tomorrow afternoon. There's a great band at Roady's. The guitarist is phenomenal." Zach smiled. If the man was more than twenty-five, it would be a fucking miracle. What the hell did he have in common with a kid that young?

"Sounds like a plan." Hawke didn't spend too much time with anyone but preferred the single men over the married ones these days. Not because he didn't like the men on his team who had spouses or children but because it just reminded him of everything he walked away from.

The only problem with that was those men he was avoiding were like family and it made for a lonely existence.

"Do you need me to pick you up?" Zach asked.

"Nope. Got Marthy back yesterday. The shop did a bang-up paint job. Thanks for the recommendation."

"That's the dumbest name for a vehicle I've ever heard. Normal people name them Betty or Betsy or Beast or something." Zach slapped him on the back. "But you're not normal."

"Neither are you," Duncan said.

Zach laughed as he strolled into the common room.

"That kid is a party animal," Duncan said. "What's cooking?"

"Ravioli." Hawke tapped his fingers on the counter.

"From a can, no doubt." Duncan shook his head. "You eat like shit."

Hawke wasn't about to argue that point, but who didn't like Chef Boyardee? Okay, the stuff tasted like cardboard doused in ketchup, but it had calories, and it would stop his stomach from growling.

"Did you hear about Wendel Lawerence?" Duncan asked.

Hawke's body tensed. "That fire still has my gut twisted. No way was it an accident and I don't believe the bullshit he's spewing." Hawke didn't know Wendel well. Only in passing. But he was one cop that Hawke didn't like. He was new to the force, fresh out of the Air Force, and his reputation was shit. "What's he up to now?"

"He's been suspended," Duncan said.

"No shit," Hawke said. "Did Kaelie finally nail him for setting the fire to his house?"

Duncan shook his head. "It's real hush-hush. But it has to do with the rape and murder of three women. I'm not sure of the details because Rusty wasn't talking. All he said was that he thinks the guy's a prick and does shitty police work. Honestly, he and Kaelie are being a little secretive about both investigations."

"That's intriguing in a bad way."

"Kaelie has Arthur, Rex, and Kent going over every detail of that fire and I hear Wendel is demanding we close it. He thinks we're stalling."

"Are we?" Hawke asked.

"No one will give me a straight answer, not even my wife, who still works part-time in Kaelie's office, so my educated guess is yes."

No sooner was dinner ready than the alarm went off. Quickly, he covered his plate and shoved it back in the fridge before making a beeline for the garage.

"We've got a jumper with a therapist sitting on the ledge with him," Chastity Booker, the dispatcher and Duncan's wife, said. "The therapist has herself strapped to the jumper."

"You've got to be kidding me?" Hawke's heart sank. This was the one call that made him question his choice in careers. They didn't happen often, but once was too many, and he'd seen a few dozen too many.

"It gets better. The jumper is an airman."

Chastity cocked a brow. "We might not be military anymore, but you can't beat that out of our blood, and we take care of our own."

"That we do." Hawke snagged the ambulance keys from the desk and settled in behind the steering wheel.

"I got the address; let's roll." Noah Hale, a fellow paramedic, hopped into the passenger seat. He'd been working with the team for the last four years and fit in nicely. Arthur had recruited him through the Air Force. Noah had a story, as they all did, but Hawke didn't know what it was. Immediately, Noah strapped himself in, then went for the GPS.

Rex Jordan jogged in front of the ambulance, tapping the hood with his helmet before shoving it on his head. "Move out," he commanded.

Hawke hit the sirens and pulled out onto the street.

"Only five miles away," Noah said. "I'd rather go help a six-hundred-pound person up off the floor or help them get out of bed than sit and cross my fingers that someone doesn't decide to go splat on the pavement."

Hawke cringed. Noah had no way of knowing his ex-girlfriend had died by suicide. The rest of his crew did and they wouldn't have dared say anything like that to him, but he'd give Noah a pass. He did what he could to bury the memories of that part of his life, but they always found him.

He headed south, following Arthur in the ladder truck and Rex in the engine.

"You're awfully quiet," Noah said.

"I hate these calls too." Hawke loved his job more than anything. When he'd first enlisted in the Air Force, he had no idea he'd end up as a firefighter, but he took to it like he'd been born with a hose in his hand. Arthur was the one who pushed him to become an EMT. Arthur needed a good combat medic on his team and wanted Hawke.

He'd been honored and signed up for the training the next day.

Gilmans Road was blocked off. Only emergency vehicles were allowed.

A local policeman moved the barricade and waved Hawke through. He parked the ambulance. As soon as his feet hit the concrete, he glanced up. The building was ten stories tall, and two people stood at the very top. He couldn't make them out, but he saw two silhouettes as clear as day.

He snagged one of the emergency bags and

went to where the rest of the team stood at the street corner.

"Do we know who's up there?" Hawke asked.

Zach handed him a pair of binoculars.

"No fucking way," he mumbled. He rubbed his eyes and blinked, but that didn't change the fact that the woman standing on the ledge next to a young man who wanted to end his life was none other than Calista Alba. Her long hair had been pulled back into a ponytail. She wore dark slacks and a yellow blouse. Thank God she'd taken off her shoes, because knowing her, she'd be wearing at least three-inch heels.

When she was dressed for work, she loved those damn fuck-me pumps. Hell, he used to love them too. But right about now, he was glad to see her toes.

Hawke clutched his chest as his fellow teammates, Garth, Kent, and Buddy, were busy opening up the chute that could potentially save Calista and her jumper. While those things served a purpose, he hated them. He'd used them more than once. And he'd been grateful for them every single time, but that didn't change all the thoughts that ran through his mind.

The biggest one was Calista had to be fucking crazy to attach herself to a jumper like that.

"Arthur. Rex. Send me up," Hawke said, standing before his boss and lieutenant. "I want to go talk to them."

"We need you down here if this goes bad." Arthur motioned to a few other firefighters.

All firemen were equipped with more than basic knowledge of first aid, but his training went way beyond that as a combat medic. He understood what his role could potentially be in this situation.

But no fucking way was he going to let Calista stand on the edge of that building a second longer.

"He's got a gun," Rex said, pointing toward the ledge with one hand while the other rested against his ear, keeping in communication with the locals on the roof. "Not only did the therapist hook herself to the young man, but now he's threatening to kill her if we use the chute."

"That's Calista Alba," Hawke said.

"Jesus fucking Christ. That's a name from the past." Rex kept his focus on the top of the building.

"Arthur, you've got to let me up there," Hawke pleaded.

"If she were the jumper, I'd say yes. But she's not. So you're staying down here," Arthur said.

"But I can help. You know what Calista and I went through. You know the drill. Come on, man, I can't stand down here and watch this shit while she's up there attached to God only knows what." Hawke paused, taking in a deep breath and swallowing the thick lump of memories that bombarded every part of his mind, body, and soul. "Together, maybe we can talk him down. She's good at her job, and I know the military."

Arthur shook his head. "I'm going up. Once I get there and assess the situation, if I think you'll be helpful, I'll let you know."

"Come on, Arthur. You can't honestly expect me to stand here and watch and wait."

But Arthur was his boss, and he called the shots. He was a smart man, and Hawke trusted him with his life.

He could trust him with Calista's.

I will honor my brothers-in-arms along with their loved ones.

Calista wasn't his woman, but she didn't deserve to die, even if she was stupid enough to strap herself to the jumper.

Hawke jogged back to the ambulance and helped Noah with the necessary medical supplies they might need. Keeping his hand over his

31

earpiece, he leaned against the vehicle and did his best to keep from losing his shit.

He folded his arms.

Then unfolded them.

He pushed himself from the cold metal and started to pace. He'd take five steps, stop, turn, and look up.

Repeat.

"Jesus Christ, will you stop?" Noah asked. "You're making me nuts."

Hawke checked his watch. They'd only been there for ten minutes.

"Jumper's name is Brad Jonson," Arthur's voice crackled over the speaker. "He spent six months in the Middle East, saw some shit, hasn't been the same since, and to pour some major salt on that wound, his girlfriend dumped him for someone else the moment he got back."

"What does he want?" Hawke covered his eyes, keeping the sun's glare from obstructing his view.

Brad held the gun in his right hand while the left one was curled around Calista's wrist. He waved the weapon in the air.

"Things look heated up there," Hawke added.

"They are. He's demanding we back off and if Dr. Alba doesn't step back inside in the next few minutes, he's taking her with him. Hawke, get your ass up here," Arthur said. "We need you to talk the good doctor into backing away. She was a little more than shocked to see me and I'm not getting through to her."

"I bet she was, and she's incredibly stubborn. On my way up." Hawke wasted no time as he raced inside the building. He punched the elevator button a dozen times. Not that it would make it come down any faster, but it gave him something to do.

The doors slid open, and there stood Arthur. "I thought I'd bring the elevator down to you."

"Thanks. Does she know I'm here?"

"Not yet, but since she saw me and Rex, it's a good guess you're on the agenda."

"She'll find out soon enough." Hawke scratched the side of his face. The memory of her palm connecting with his cheek burned his skin.

No regrets.

Right. No matter how many times he pushed that mantra down his own throat, he choked on it. The only thing he didn't regret was leaving the Air Force and following Arthur to Jacksonville, Florida.

He rolled his neck, flexing his biceps, preparing for… he had no idea. A half dozen first responders were gathered near a broken window. He took a quick glance around, wondering if this was Calista's office. He had no idea what she'd done with her life. Not once had he returned to his hometown or Dover. There had been no reason to since his parents had passed. And he never looked her up.

Calista sent him a letter or two to his brother's house every year, and Hawke put them in a box.

Unopened.

Unread.

He dared not even look at the return address, always covering it with his thumb. Why he kept the damn things, he had no idea. Then again, he didn't know why he had kept a copy of Courtney's suicide note, other than to read it every once in a while, reminding him of what he'd caused.

His brother constantly told him to read Calista's letters and reach out. That he'd been a total prick for how he left.

He'd always respond with, *Tell me something I don't know.*

"Two minutes, Dr. Alba," a male voice commanded. "Don't make me do this."

Hawke had seen more than one person take their own life. Thankfully, he went on more calls that didn't end with death, but he'd come to learn to recognize when a person was serious, and this man would kill Calista, no doubt about that.

"I'm not making you do anything. I'm asking you to come inside and try for one more day." Calista's voice ignited a flash of heat that rippled over his body. Anger and love collided as if in a high-speed crash, leaving no survivors.

"I do that, and these assholes will arrest me. I'm not spending any more time in a cage. I'm done," the man said.

"I don't blame you," Hawke said as he stuck his head out the window.

Calista turned, and her jaw dropped open. Her eyes widened with shock but quickly narrowed into tiny, angry slits.

He couldn't blame her either.

"Who the fuck are you?" Brad pushed the gun against Calista's temple.

"I'm an old friend of your therapist." All he needed to do was ensure that Brad's gaze was stuck on him and not on what was going on below. "I'm here to beg her to step back inside so you can go about doing whatever you want to do with your life."

"I'm not going to let you jump," Calista said. "And you're not a killer."

"Yes, I am," Brad said.

"Combat doesn't count," Calista said.

"Actually, it does." Hawke's heart pounded in his chest. He didn't want his kind to die. He understood what war could do to a man, and there was hope.

There was always hope.

Something Courtney refused to consider.

Calista glared.

"But this would be different than what you had to do for this country. Calista is only trying to help you, something you pay her to do."

"What the hell do you know about war?" Brad asked.

"I did three tours in the Middle East when I was in the Air Force. I still have nightmares sometimes, but the need to lock myself in a closet so I can cry like a baby is long gone. Calista, undo the belt, please."

"I can't just let him—"

"You're not. We're trading places. Military take care of their own." He stepped out on the ledge, even though Arthur and Rex were yelling at him through the earpiece. "Do it, Calista. Now."

The men below had the chute ready, just in case.

Calista released the belt with a shaking hand, holding her to Brad. She placed her hand in Hawke's.

Pop!

"No!"

Hawke grabbed hold of Calista and shoved her through the window, right into Arthur's arms. Tightly holding on to the side of the building, he glanced toward the pavement. His team had caught Brad in the chute, and Noah was kneeling over him, checking for vitals.

"We've got a pulse," Noah's voice boomed in Hawke's ear.

"I've got to get back down there." He stepped off the ledge and stopped in front of Calista. He reached out and brushed a chunk of hair that had fallen out of her ponytail. "He's still alive."

"Thank you," she said.

"Just doing my job."

"You didn't have to—"

"Yeah. I did. We're taking him to the local hospital. My boss here will fill you in and you can follow us, if he survives." He let out a puff of air. "That was insanely stupid what you did. That man could have killed you."

She poked his chest. "This is my job. I know what I'm doing."

"No. This is my job. Your job is to sit on that sofa over there and listen to people. Not walk out on a ledge and offer to die with them."

"Oh, that's rich. Isn't that what you were doing when you decided to switch places?"

"My team was inflating the chute. Besides, my role was to get your ass back inside and deal with him once that was done." He raked his hand through his hair. "What you did was reckless and stupid." With that, he turned on his heel and marched out of the office and, hopefully, right out of her life again.

Calista raced through the halls of the hospital. She wouldn't let Hawke run off again like they had nothing to discuss.

Not until she had a chance to tell him what a fucking asshole he was and that he'd never, ever see his son. She didn't give a shit about what he'd said in her office. Or that he'd insulted her in front of his colleagues. She couldn't care less what he thought about *her* actions. It was his that were questionable.

She slowed to a snail's pace as she pushed open the bay doors where the ambulances brought patients. The humid Florida heat smacked her face like scalding hot water.

Did she really want to confront him? She'd sent him letters and pictures every year. He had every chance to meet his son and be a part of his life, but he chose not to.

How she could have ever loved him was a mystery.

Why she still loved him was insanity.

The ambulance he'd driven was still parked in the lot to the side of the drop-off circle. He sat on the back edge, his phone in his hands, finger tapping away on the screen.

Jerk hadn't changed a bit. His sandy-brown hair had been cut short, just like his military days, but his five o'clock shadow had already started to dot his face. She'd always found that to be sexy. He'd been fit ten years ago, but damn, his biceps looked like they were hard as a rock and so much more defined than before.

And those bright, piercing blue eyes stole her breath.

Her heels clicked on the pavement. The noise must have caught his attention since he lifted his head.

He stood, waving his cell out in front of him. "I was just trying to find your contact information off the internet. You're not an easy person to find. You don't seem to be listed anywhere. I wanted to make sure you were okay."

"Right. Or maybe you just wanted to ream me a new asshole again." She nearly choked on her laugh. "You knew I was in the hospital. You could have just come in and found me." Tension kneaded its ugly fingers into her shoulders and jaw.

He scratched at the side of his face. "Last time I saw you, you left a handprint, and I didn't want to risk it, especially after what I said, which was in the heat of the moment. I shouldn't have said all that and I'm sorry."

"Well, the good news is I'm not going to slap you, but I do get to call you a douchebag to your face."

To his credit, he stood there like a man, staring her in the eye. Something he hadn't done ten years ago.

"I've been called worse." He nodded.

"How could you?" she asked.

"How could I what? Leave you ten years ago? I think I explained myself at Courtney's grave."

"Not what I'm talking about and you know it." She planted her hands on her hips. God, hitting him right now would feel so good. This wasn't the man she'd fallen in love with. His anger lifted off his skin like steam from a hot spring. The therapist in her knew he still carried every ounce of guilt he felt all those years ago. It had to be slowly killing him, and a tiny piece of her wanted to help him.

The rest of her, however, wanted to hurt him like no one else ever has so he could feel just a little bit of what it's been like for her and her son for the last ten years. Wilson constantly asked questions about his father, and she was running out of lies.

He raised his palms toward the sky. "Calista, I really don't know what you're talking about. But since we're standing here, I'm sorry I was a prick. I shouldn't have left that way. If I could go back in time, I'd change how I called it quits."

"Seriously? You're going to apologize for that, of all things? I know you got my letters. Your brother told me he sends every single one." She couldn't care less about how he broke up with her.

"I didn't read them."

"What?" Tears welled in her eyes. Her stomach clenched and twisted, threatening to regurgitate what she'd eaten for lunch, which wasn't so good going down, so she could only imagine what it would be like coming up. "What did you do with them? Throw them away?" Instinctively, she clutched her locket, thumbing the silver clasp that held the picture of Wilson Hawke Alba. All these years, she believed Hawke had wanted nothing to do with his son. Only it was her he was running from. He had never cared enough for her, even to open one damn letter.

Selfish asshole.

And *her* son had paid the price.

Hawke glanced over his shoulder before catching her gaze. He held her stare for a long minute. His facial muscles didn't flinch at all.

She hated not being able to read him. Not even his ice-blue eyes gave anything away.

"I have them." His voice remained flat, unemotional, and undetached, much like he had ten years ago. It was as if Courtney had taken him to the grave with her. "I've just never wanted to read them. I can't go back to that time and we really don't have anything left to say to one another. I'm sorry."

Dropping her hands to her sides, she sucked in a deep breath. "I'm not asking you to go back." She dug her hand into her cross-body purse and pulled out a business card. "I want nothing from you. I feel nothing for you anymore. That all died the day we buried Courtney and you chose a different path. One that didn't include me." She hadn't said that name in years, and it tripped over her tongue and tumbled out of her mouth in a freefall. She cleared her throat and held up a finger. "I have one thing to ask of you. Just one. And it's really fucking important, so I need you to do it."

"What's that?"

"Read the letters. I've sent you a couple a year for the last ten. They aren't long, except the first one. You don't need to call me or ever speak to me again, but do me the favor of taking the time—"

"Why don't you just tell me what's in them or what's so important that you had to keep writing."

She shook her head. The nerve of that man. She'd given him the choice, but he hadn't bothered to even peek in one envelope.

No way could she handle looking him in the eye

43

and telling him he had an almost ten-year-old son. He'd either be devastated he'd lost ten years of his boy's life or angry that she even thought he'd care. Either way, she didn't want to be beside him when he found out. Besides, he lost that privilege when he dodged her right before he left the military. Odd that they both ended up in the same city and didn't know it.

"Why not?" he asked.

"I have a million reasons, but the biggest one is you lost the right to ask anything of me the second you chose to walk out of my life. Read the letters, and then we'll talk. Or don't read the letters. That's your choice. I've got to go." She turned on her heel.

Thick, long fingers curled around her arm. The familiar sensation of his warmth sent her down a road she thought she'd long forgotten. Hot blood pumped through her veins, reminding her of a love so great that no man has ever been able to fill it.

"Now who's walking away?"

She jerked, trying to yank herself free from his tight grasp so she could rid herself of all the emotions she tried to tell herself had been crushed the day he left her standing over Courtney's coffin.

"Just tell me." His nostrils flared like a frustrated

bull waiting to charge. "What's the big deal if I read it or hear it."

She swiped at her cheeks, resenting the waterfall pouring from her eyes. Her life had never been easy. Her father had died in jail when she'd been in high school, and her mother died of a drug overdose about the same time she started dating Hawke. He'd lost his mother to cancer, and his father died in the line of duty right after he'd graduated from the Air Force Academy, so he understood some of what she went through. He'd been so kind to her all through school, knowing what her home life was like where the rest of the kids shunned her.

"What's in the letters?" His strong hands rested on her shoulders.

"You asked me not to chase after you, and other than one time, I respected that. However, I took the time to write you. You can take the time to read them. Like I said, we never have to see each other again if that is what you want."

His calloused hands ran up and down her arms five times before he dropped them to his sides. "When I saw you on the ledge of that building, my heart sank. I couldn't believe that you were risking your life that way. It reminded me of the time we found Courtney with a handful of pills, and it brought everything back, and I couldn't push it away. Maybe we could have lunch sometime so we can talk, something we should have done before I left."

All of this was a little too late, yet she owed it to her son to give Hawke a chance. But she couldn't bring herself to say the words to his face.

Or maybe she wanted to torture him.

Either way, before they had an in-depth conversation about the subject, she needed him to accept what he'd turned his back on. "I'll meet you for lunch, but only if you read the letters." She raised up on tiptoe and kissed his cheek, letting her lips linger to taste his salty skin. "My number is in those letters."

"You look good. Real good," he said as his lips curled into a smile.

"You look like you've spent a lifetime running from the past, but it looks like the past just caught up with you. Deal with it, or you'll end up a very lonely, sad man." She suspected he was already there; he just hadn't accepted it. "I hope I hear from you."

"I'm on duty until tomorrow morning, so I won't be able to read them until after I get off work."

"I'll talk to you later." With her heart hammering in her chest, she turned and made her way back into the hospital.

Wilson was either going to have his father.

Or she was going to have to break her son's heart.

2

*H*awke tossed his keys on the kitchen counter. He'd rented this house for the last two years, and he loved the neighborhood, in part because it wasn't close to any of the married men on his team. When he'd first moved to Jacksonville, they all lived within five miles of each other, except Rex.

That man spent the first year on his boat.

But as time passed, and each of his crew fell in love and started a family, they either moved or their wives moved in with them.

It got to be more than Hawke could bear. So, he found a place close to the beach and between the fire station and the Aegis Network. Zach and Noah lived on the other side of the street. A few other firefighters on another team also lived nearby. They were also single, which was nice when he wanted to kick back and have a beer.

But mostly, Hawke didn't like to socialize much anymore. It wasn't that he didn't like the other firemen, he did. However, they weren't Arthur and the other guys and frankly, he missed them. He missed the old days.

Now all he had was work.

Other than his brother, he had no family left.

His team was his family, but those men had families of their own to take care of and honor. Hawke understood that.

Seeing Calista again only stirred up things he'd rather never experience again. The moment he'd held her by the forearms, staring into her eyes, every emotion he'd ever felt for the woman came barreling down on him like a rocket reentering the earth's atmosphere. Fiery, bumpy, and out of control.

He snagged a glass of orange juice before heading back to the bedroom. The place had three: one he obviously used for sleeping, one he used for an office, which came in handy for his work with the Aegis Network, and the third was used as a guest room, though only one person had spent the night there.

His brother.

And that had been a month ago when he stopped by unexpectedly after a grueling mission with another letter from Calista. Colt also gave Hawke quite the lecture about avoidance. As if Colt knew anything. The man had no idea what the word commitment meant unless it was attached to a re-signing bonus. Colt loved the military more than he loved women, and he enjoyed the company of many.

Hawke set the glass on the bathroom sink and splashed his face with water. He leaned over and stared at his reflection. Deep wrinkles had started to form around his eyes, but it was the lack of any life behind them that haunted him.

"Open the damn letters." He went to the office. Opening the closet door, he pulled out the box labeled: CA.

Calista Alba.

He sat down at the small, dark wooden desk that faced the window. He could see Noah and Zach's house. A few of the single men were sitting in the backyard, drinking a few beers, waiting until they were so tired that their bodies wouldn't care that it was nine in the morning. They would sleep on and off for the next day, recovering from an overnight shift.

He could get on board with a mind-numbing beer or two, but Calista was right. He at least owed it to her to read the letters. He could do that for her.

But where to start?

He pulled out the first letter and read the return address. She'd still been living in Dover, Delaware, when she sent that one.

He set it aside and decided to start with the last one. Taking the old-fashioned letter opener his mother left him, he carefully tore through the envelope. A picture fell to the desk.

He held the image in his trembling hands, staring into the hauntingly familiar blue eyes of a young boy, maybe nine, holding a fishing pole.

The picture burned his fingertips. He tossed it aside and opened the letter.

Dear Hawke,

I know this isn't when I normally write. But I've got news and I thought you should know. I'm moving again. My marriage fell apart.

He rubbed his stinging eyes. She'd moved on.

Had a family. He was sorry it hadn't worked out for her, but he was glad she'd left him in the past.

That had been the right thing to do.

I don't know why I got married. Maybe it was because I felt like Wilson needed a father figure.

"What the fuck," he mumbled, snagging the picture again. She named her fucking kid with his last name. Why?

Only, deep down, Hawke knew why. He just didn't want to admit it. Not this second, anyway.

But Doug wasn't much of that. He had two kids of his own he needed to make time for and blending our families didn't work. Besides, I don't think I loved him.

Not like I loved you.

You ruined me, in more ways than one. Oh. I don't blame you anymore. Not for that. I'm a big girl and can take responsibility for the outcome of my own life. But Wilson is an innocent child, and he has so many questions. I keep telling him that his father was an important man. A firefighter and combat medic in the Air Force when I knew him, even though he retired shortly after our relationship ended.

I figured since you never returned a single letter, you didn't want anyone to know you were a father.

His heart raced so fast he couldn't feel when one beat started and the other ended.

A father.

He was a father.

He had a son.

He slammed his fist on the desk, sending the stack of envelopes to the ground. They scattered about the floor.

"Fuck." There had to be at least thirty letters.

And more pictures.

He dropped to the floor. Sitting cross-legged, he arranged the letters by order of postmark.

Two or three letters a year. One around Christmas. One around Halloween.

The third grouping of letters was postmarked on the same date every year.

May 29.

Today was April 8.

With trembling hands, he held the last letter in front of his face.

I don't know why I keep writing to you. I keep thinking that maybe this thing you followed Arthur to has you jumping from one place to the next. I have no idea. You never told me the name of the organization. We never got that far. It was all what-if talk—nothing concrete until you left me standing there with a broken heart. But you're not in the military anymore, so I don't know.

Your son will be ten this May.

Part of me thinks I should stop this altogether. I wonder

if I'm hurting our son. Giving him false hope that you will come to him. Love him. I want to hang on to that, but then the realist in me kicks in and maybe now I need to end this. Maybe this will finally be the last letter. Maybe it's time for me to accept that when you walked away from me, you walked away from Wilson, too.

"Jesus Christ." He flipped through the envelopes until he found the one postmarked May 29, ten years ago. Without using the metal letter opener, he fumbled with the paper, praying he didn't destroy any image of *his* son. He let the letter fall to his lap and held up a picture of Calista, in a hospital bed, with a naked newborn on her chest.

Her dark hair was piled on top of her head. A few curls curved down the side of her face. Her sweet lips pressed against the baby's forehead. The boy looked to be a good size. His pink skin glowed against Calista. His tiny fingers wrapped around her thumb.

A single tear fell from Hawke's right eye.

He took the letter from his lap and held it into the sunlight streaming through the window.

Dear Hawke,

I hope you received the last couple of letters. I've asked Colt a million times where you went after you left the Air Force, but he won't tell me shit. He says that's for you to tell me, but I haven't heard anything. For all I know, you re-enlisted. But something in the way Colt's expression changed when I asked that question tells me otherwise. I wish I knew how to reach you so I don't have to keep going through Colt. And I don't understand why you haven't responded. I know the kind of man you are—caring and kind.

Hawke held the picture up in his other hand. He wondered if Calista had gone through child-birth alone or if someone had been by her side. Who helped her raise their son? Knowing Calista, the strong, stubborn, independent woman that she was, she probably did it all by herself.

Until she got married.

His heart squeezed so tight he had to clutch his chest. Another man had been married to Calista and had played a role in *his* son's life.

I wish I had known I was pregnant for sure that day at the cemetery. As I wrote in my last letter, I hoped we could take the test together. But I didn't think that day was the right day to say, hey, Hawke, remember when the condom broke? Well, yeah, I think I'm going to have a baby.

I tried to get in touch with you. I want you to know your son. I don't care if you don't want anything to do with me. I can live with that.

But you need your son, and he needs you.

By the way, I named him Wilson Hawke Alba. You are

listed as the father on his birth certificate. I know, when you come back, and if we give him your last name, which I'm perfectly fine with, he might be in a pickle as Wilson Hawke Wilson, but we can just call him Hawke, or change his first name.

What was I thinking?

I'm going to call him Hawke.

"But you called him Wilson in this last letter." Hawke scratched the side of his face. Not a day went by that he didn't remember that slap. It had left a red mark for two days. But he had deserved more.

And his son deserved better.

You should know that this little fella wasn't so little, weighing in at nine pounds eight ounces and twenty-two inches long. Thank God it was a quick delivery. I almost gave birth in the elevator on the way in. He came so fast it was frightening, but I had a friend from work with me.

I would have rather had you.

Below is my address and cell number. Looking forward to introducing you to your son.

Love, Calista.

He tore through the rest of the envelopes, ignoring the letters and focusing on each and every detail of his son. Every year, he changed so much.

She had sent him pictures of him walking,

sitting on the potty with a book, and playing in the sandbox.

He gasped, holding a group of images of his son playing in his first soccer game. Another one of him holding a golf club.

But his favorite had to be of him on the ski slopes. His son's piercing blue eyes danced with mischief in the sun. It looked as if they had lived up north for a bit.

He found two letters with postmarks from Vermont and unfolded the one from Christmastime.

Dear Hawke,

I promised myself I'd never keep your son from you, but it seems you don't want him. Maybe I'm sending these to hurt you. Or maybe to hurt myself for thinking you'd actually want to be a father.

My mistake.

I got married a couple of months ago when my boyfriend took a job in Vermont. God, I hate it here. Too much snow and cold. You'd think I'd be used to it, considering where we grew up and where I went to college, but Doug, my husband, is from here, so it's nice to have a family. And Wilson has stepsiblings to play with. It's a good life for him.

He has so many questions about you, but I'm at the point

where I think I need to either tell him you're dead or crush his little heart and tell him the truth.

You don't want him.

Hawke jumped to his feet and kicked the chair. "Of course I want him. I just didn't know he fucking existed." If he was being honest, he wanted her too.

But that wasn't something he'd contemplate. Not now. Not ever. He'd let her go for a reason. A good one. And there was no going back.

Ding-dong.

He jumped.

Racing toward the front door, clutching the picture of Wilson on the ski slopes in his hand, he hoped—no—he prayed the person standing on the other side would be Calista.

And Wilson.

He pulled back the door and groaned. "Hey, Duncan. What are you doing here?"

Duncan held up a six-pack. "Chastity heard you knew the therapist on the ledge and told me I had to come over. I told her I knew her too and that you needed some space, but she wasn't hearing any of it. She kicked me right in the ass and told me to text as soon as I got here."

"I thought she was working with Kaelie today."

Hawke shoved the picture in his back pocket with a shaky hand. His mind was still reeling from the news. But he wouldn't dare push his friend out the door. He had no valid reason, and Duncan had been there when Courtney died. He'd been a great source of comfort to Hawke, and right now, Hawke needed a friend.

Duncan was part of what he called the married crew. Arthur, Rex, Kent, Buddy, Duncan, and Garth. All of them had children except Garth, but his wife was expecting. It was like there was something in the water at the firehouse. They were all pumping out babies faster than a speeding bullet.

"Nope. Her folks are visiting, so she's taking them and the kids to the zoo. Since she knows a little bit about your history," Duncan said with a weak smile, "she thought I should head over and see how you were doing."

"For Mennonites, her parents are very cool." Hawke decided to leave the last comment alone. He knew his crew meant well, and these calls affected him deeply.

"They are the best. And the kids adore them, which is even better." Duncan waved the six-pack in the air. "Are you going to let me in or what?"

"I'm surprised Arthur, Rex, and everyone else

aren't with you." Hawke took the beer and headed toward the kitchen, contemplating whether or not he would indulge. He needed to call Calista, but he hadn't figured out what to say. He was pissed. Actually, that didn't even begin to cover his emotions. She'd been in contact with his brother. Colt knew how to reach him. She could have sent him a message saying that it was imperative that she speak with him and he might have taken her call.

Of course, she could have told his brother. Granted, Colt had been instructed to stay the fuck out of it. Hawke had ended it with Calista, and no matter what, he didn't want to hear anything that could come out of her mouth. No pleading. No begging. Because there was nothing she could say or do that would change his mind.

Knowing his brother, he'd put duct tape around her mouth before he'd break a promise to Hawke and sit and listen to her words.

"Arthur and Rex were pretty torked I stepped out on the ledge, especially considering what happened in the past and my connection to Calista. They thought I was the one being reckless."

"Wasn't the brightest thing you ever did, but you got the job done, and no one died."

Hawke had been keeping a more considerable distance between him, all the married men on the team, and their families lately. He tried to avoid going to their barbeques or other family gatherings, even when Noah, his paramedic partner, or other firefighters who weren't married went. Being around families always made him uncomfortable. Not just because he didn't think he wanted one anymore, but it always reminded him of the day he walked away from Calista.

He loved his crew like family, but as each one fell in love and tied the knot, he pulled away, and his brothers-in-arms kept trying to suck him back in. He wanted them in his life. Wanted it to go back to how it was when they were in the Air Force. Bachelors. Free and living the dream.

He'd never felt so alone in his life.

And now he just found out he was a father.

"I've done dumber," Hawke said.

"We all have." Duncan nodded. "But the real issue is, are you going to talk about this? About Calista's return? Or are you going to pull further away?"

Hawke twisted off the cap from two longnecks before shoving the rest in the fridge. He handed one to his buddy who sat on the stool at the counter in the kitchen. Both men sipped their beers in deafening silence.

Duncan was a patient man—maybe a little too patient. Hawke always assumed it stemmed from his religious background, and perhaps it did, but Duncan also had a calmness about him that served him well when he ran into burning buildings or was on a mission. He also had an uncanny ability to put people at ease no matter the situation.

"Is everyone on the team talking about the fact that Calista is in town and what happened to Courtney?"

"It's not like that, man," Duncan said. "We've been down this road with you before. We all know how you get, but lately, you've been more withdrawn than usual. It's worsened since Garth got married and announced he and Amber were having a baby."

"I'm happy for Garth. For everyone."

"Never said you weren't. But I can't imagine what it's like for you to see Calista again. None of us know the whole story. And maybe we don't need to know, but your reaction to her was a little over the top." Duncan raised his hand. "We all understand that at one time you cared a great deal for her, but your words were not only unkind but unprofessional in that setting."

"I know, and I've apologized, but the details surrounding what happened in the past aren't overly complicated and you do know most of it," Hawke said. "When I met you guys, you all had been working together for a while. I came on the team last after graduating from the Academy and doing fire school. My on-and-off relationship with Courtney had ended, so you guys didn't see most of that. We'd been broken up for a while, but she wouldn't let go. She followed me to Dover, which was where Calista lived. Courtney said it was for a job, but it was a lie. Then she said it was to be near Calista, but that wasn't true either. It was for me. She would call me in the middle of the night, telling me she had nothing to live for. I'd race over to take care of her. Most of the time it was idle threats, but I always knew she was capable of taking her own life." Hawke raised his beer to his lips. The bubbles fought their way down his throat, hitting his stomach like a cement rock. "Calista was her best friend."

"So far, you haven't told me anything I don't know," Duncan said.

Hawke nodded, but he needed to tell the story.

He needed to hear and feel the words roll off his tongue. It wasn't to make sense of it, because no one could do that. But perhaps to clear his mind of everything so he could face Calista.

And his young son.

"Calista and I kept it secret, which was stupid. But I thought it was better if Courtney didn't find out. I don't know what I was thinking. I was twenty-eight. A grown man. I should have known better. At the time, I thought Courtney would eventually ease up. But she never did, and one day she showed up at Calista's place and found us in bed. That was the beginning of the end. Things just escalated."

"That part, we didn't know. Why didn't you tell us what happened and how the hell did she get in?"

"She had a key." Hawke pushed his beer aside. If he drank another drop, he'd puke his guts out. "Courtney had made one without Calista's knowledge and I didn't say anything because we were being deployed two days later on Operation Firebrand. I had to focus on work. When I returned, Courtney started in on her antics. I guess part of me was embarrassed and I didn't want to burden anyone."

"We're family. This is what we're here for. It's

no different than all the shit you've been around for all of us. But what Courtney did was criminal."

"Courtney did a lot of crazy things. I did care about her, so I always raced to her side whenever she said she might cause herself harm."

"I'm sorry, man," Duncan said. "It's not your fault."

"But she blamed me in her suicide note." Hawke ran a hand over his face. He still had that damn note, and he constantly pulled it out and read it as if to torture himself. But as he lay in his bunk at the fire station half the night, he thought about the airman and who he might blame for why he wanted to die.

The Air Force?

War?

The woman who cheated on him?

Calista?

There was so much pain in that man's eyes and all he wanted to do was find a way to end it. Taking his own life wasn't the answer. Sure, it would end it, but not for those he loved.

"You never told me she left a note, much less blamed you. And dude, that doesn't make it your fault. Or Calista's."

"Hang on a sec." Hawke slipped from the kitchen and back into the office, where he gathered all the pictures and letters from Calista and stuffed them back into the box. Opening the desk drawer, he flipped open a little container and pulled out his copy of the note. He tucked the box under his arm and marched back to the kitchen. Never in a million years did he think he'd talk to a single soul about this stuff.

Especially not to one of the married crew.

Hell, he hadn't even spoken to his brother about it much over the years. It was just too damn painful.

But knowing he had a son, well that changed everything.

He set the box on the counter and unfolded the note. "Just listen, and then you tell me if you wouldn't blame yourself after reading it."

"To whom it may concern.

Because it concerns no one.

No one cares. If they cared, they would have picked up the phone. But Hawke didn't. He ignored me for her, and she did the same. They only care about each other. I'm not even an afterthought anymore.

All I wanted to ask was why? Why didn't they tell me? Maybe if I had known they were a couple and wanted to move in together, I might have started to let go of Hawke. I held on so tight because I loved him. And at one point, he loved me.

But that changed.

Just like with my parents.

They couldn't be bothered with me either.

I'm tired. And I'm done. There is nothing and no one left for me.

Loving someone hurts too much, and I can't make it stop while I'm alive. Hawke once told me that love is all we have to look forward to. I looked forward to so much with him— the life we planned together—but he destroyed it. He destroyed me. All he had to do was be honest, but instead, he lied to my face.

Why? He always demanded the truth from me, but I guess that doesn't work both ways.

I believed in him. In love. Until he broke my heart into a million pieces. I can't put it back together so I'm going to put it out of its misery.

To whom it may concern.

Or not.

Goodbye."

"I get it. That would tear me apart. But those are the words of a woman in pain and she wanted someone else to feel that too. She needed therapy," Duncan said. "We've seen it many times on the job, but she made that choice, not you."

"I know she needed counseling. But Courtney hung herself within a half hour of when she called me and I didn't answer. All I needed to do was pick up that damn phone."

"You can't be expected to take every call. Not from an ex-girlfriend. Especially not one who made your life miserable, and come on, man, that's exactly what Courtney did. She followed you to the point it would be considered stalking by any legal standing." Duncan had a valid point, one Hawke knew was true. He couldn't deny that any longer.

Reading that note out loud and yesterday's events put more than one thing in perspective.

"Seeing that jumper yesterday. Watching him shoot himself the second Calista undid the belt that held them together made me realize no matter what I had done differently with Courtney, without proper help, she probably would have done the same thing. If not that time, another time. I know that. She used me in her life as her reason to be miserable. If not me, it would have been someone else. She did that in her death. She could have focused her energy on Calista. She betrayed Courtney too. But instead, she chose me. I do get that. I can intellectually see that it's not my fault even if my heart wants to believe otherwise."

"I'm honestly glad to hear you say that. Arthur and Rex were pretty worried about you, and I hope you don't mind me saying you have kept us at arm's length these last few years, and it's annoying as fuck. We used to be so close. We're a team. Family. That's why Arthur wouldn't let you go when you put in for a transfer. You belong here. With us."

"I've struggled with that for a while now. It's not any of you. It's me, and today, I learned something that has me even more screwed up in the head than before." He pulled the picture out of his pocket and glanced at it. His son's smile was spread wide across his face. "This was taken a few years ago, but right before you rang that bell, I discovered I'm a father."

Duncan dropped his beer on the floor. His mouth hung wide open as the bottle smashed against the tile. He took the image in his hands. "Christ. He looks just like you."

"It's like looking into a mirror at the past. And there's more." Hawke carefully cleaned up the mess while Duncan sorted through all the pictures. Hawke was used to long silences between him and the team. Everyone, even when kept at an emotional distance, had that same need for quiet retrospection.

"She kept him from you," Duncan said as more of a statement than a question.

"No. She wrote me all these letters, but I didn't open them until I got home from work." Hawke dumped the broken glass in the trash and cleaned the floor with a wet rag.

"That makes you about the biggest asshole I've ever met." Duncan shook his head.

Leave it to one of his brothers-in-arms to call the kettle black.

"It's not like I planned on being a prick. The question is, what do I do now? She's just off a divorce, and I have no idea if that man is still in my son's life. Or what he knows or thinks of me. I sure as shit don't want to upset the boy or disrupt his home life. But I want to know him. I want to take him fishing. What else does enjoy besides that and skiing? Does he like to read? Is he into video games? Sports? I don't know one fucking thing about this kid except he looks exactly like me at that age."

"Hawke. Slow down and take a breath. One thing at a time, and you should start with calling the boy's mother and having a conversation." Duncan grabbed a fresh beer and raised it. "Unless you've already done that?"

"Nope." Hawke hadn't ever felt he needed anyone to hold his hand. Whatever happened in his life, he handled it alone. He'd spent the last ten years numb. He ran into burning buildings without a second thought. He did his best to save people's lives. He jumped from one assignment to the next with the Aegis Network, not out of a need to keep busy but out of fear of making connections. He'd left the one person he'd loved with all his soul behind, and with her, he left his heart. "I hate to ask this, but would you mind taking a drive with me? I found out she lives just a couple of neighborhoods north of here."

Duncan stood and eased around the side of the island, slapping his hand against Hawke's back. "It's about time you leaned on your family."

"Interesting choice of words."

Duncan smiled. "I love my wife and kids. They are everything to me. But this team that I call my brothers, they are a different kind of family. We understand each other in ways that our families don't—well, everyone else's wife but mine, since she's one of us."

"That is the weirdest thing you've ever said."

"But you get where I'm going with it. We are here for each other no matter what. So if you need me to have your back, I'll do it as long as it's not while you're taking a piss."

For the first time in many years, Hawke felt like he belonged again. It wasn't about fitting in, but about opening up his heart and soul and allowing someone to care about him.

That maybe, he actually deserved it.

alista rarely canceled on her patients, but she needed a few days to collect herself. Between Brad trying to kill himself and her, and the cleanup in her office, she deserved a break.

Not to mention seeing Hawke. She had no idea he'd been living in Florida, although, it shouldn't have surprised her because he loved the ocean. He loved being in the sun. It was his kind of place. However, she might have picked Texas to relocate if she had known. That was even farther from the great maple state of Vermont. Speaking of syrup, she slathered her son's pancakes in the sticky stuff. Deep down, she knew that marriage wouldn't last, but she did it anyway. She wanted a family for her son. Stability. Dumb reason to get married.

Doug was nice enough. Attentive enough.

But he wasn't Hawke.

And she couldn't give herself to Doug completely when her heart was still with the man who ripped it from her chest and tossed it aside like rotten eggs.

"Wilson. Let's hurry up. The school bus will be here in fifteen minutes."

"Coming, Mom!"

Five seconds later, her son skidded to a stop in front of the kitchen table. She'd rented a small house in Ocean Side Village. It was a nice community with lots of families. There were plenty of kids Wilson's age to play with and she loved that for her son.

It would be good for a year while she looked for a place to buy.

She ruffled Wilson's soft hair. It was a little lighter than Hawke's, but other than that, there was no mistaking who Wilson's father was. She glanced over her shoulder to the picture of Hawke she always kept on the fridge. It was one of her favorite images. He wore loose-fitting jeans and a black V-neck shirt. He leaned against his truck, arms folded across his chest. He sported a huge smile. The one that made her knees go weak every time she dared to stare at the picture for more than a second. It was taken right before Courtney had killed herself. Hawke had just come home from having been deployed for three weeks and Calista had been so happy to see him. He'd presented his dilemma to her regarding the rest of the team wanting to leave the Air Force, a career he loved, and he was so torn. He had no idea what to do, until the day Courtney died.

That changed everything.

"Eat up, kiddo." She sat across from Wilson with a hot cup of coffee. The steam rose up to her nostrils, and she inhaled the rich scent of mocha, cream, and splash of cinnamon.

"What will you do today since you're not working?" Wilson asked.

"I thought I'd catch up on some of my shows and maybe read a book." She palmed the mug and took a small sip. Relaxing would be out of the question, even though she planned on trying.

Only, she'd be pacing with her cell in her hand, waiting for Hawke to call.

If he called.

"That sounds so boring. You should play some video games or maybe go outside and kick a ball around." Wilson raised a forkful of pancakes and stuffed it in his mouth. Syrup dribbled down his cheek. He swiped at it with the back of his hand.

Snagging a napkin, she reached across the table.

"Mom!" He took it from her hand and cleaned off his face. "I'm not a little kid anymore. I'm almost in double digits." He sat a little taller and smiled.

Just like his father.

"Yes, you are, but you'll always be my little boy."

Wilson rolled his eyes.

She watched her precious child devour his breakfast. The last ten years had gone by too fast.

"Go brush your teeth. We've got five minutes." She tapped her Apple Watch.

"Yes, ma'am." Wilson pushed back from the table, taking his plate with him. He paused in front of the fridge. "Are you still looking for my dad?"

"Every day." She swallowed. If Hawke wanted nothing to do with his son, then she'd bite the bullet and lie to her kid that his father had been killed. He was a firefighter, and now she knew he worked for a private security firm that did missions similar to the military. He could have died any number of ways. What other choice did she have? She knew the truth would probably come out, but not until Wilson was an adult and had the skill set to understand that his father's decision had nothing to do with him.

"Why is it so hard to find him? Can't we ask the Air Force where he went after he left? Or do searches in fire departments in each state?" Wilson dumped his plate in the sink and faced her with tears welling in his eyes.

Her heart sank into the pit of her stomach. She'd had this conversation a million times with Wilson. When she'd given birth, she ran on the assumption that Hawke just hadn't gotten her letters yet. She let that thought rule her for the next two years when reality had sunk in, and Hawke hadn't returned a single letter, and she knew for damn sure he'd gotten them.

Telling Wilson about his father's identity had been a mistake. It didn't matter that her only intention had been to make sure Wilson didn't go through life thinking he was a bastard. That if his father knew about his existence, he'd be in his life.

"Sweetheart. We've been over this. The Air Force doesn't keep track of where people go after they leave the military, and there is no national database for firefighters. It's like finding a needle in a haystack. I'm doing the best I can, kiddo."

"Why didn't you tell him about me before he

left the military?" Wilson's lower lip quivered. "Before he left Dover."

She knew from experience that this line of questioning wasn't going to end in the next few minutes, so she reconciled that she'd be driving her son to school today. And that was okay. He could be late.

Hell, he was in the fourth grade. He could take the day off. It's not like he missed much school. Perhaps it would be good for them to spend the day together. It would certainly get her mind off of waiting for Hawke to read her letters. And if he did open them, he'd need some time to digest the information.

"Come here." She patted her leg.

Wilson didn't sit on her lap often anymore, but he didn't hesitate this time.

"I didn't know about you until after your father decided to leave the Air Force. Our relationship had ended and he was deployed. I never saw him again. But as soon as I learned I was having you, I started searching for him." That wasn't a lie. "I wish I could tell you I knew where he was or what he was doing, but I can't."

"Do you think he died on that mission?" Wilson had asked this question many times, and she'd always given him the same answer.

Before she could answer, her cell phone rang. She raised her arm, glancing at the number flashing on her Apple Watch. She had no idea who it was, so she'd let it go to voicemail.

"It's possible."

Ding-dong.

"I hope he's okay." Wilson wiped his face and leaped from her lap. "I'll get it."

"I love you, kiddo. You're the best thing that has ever happened to me."

Wilson flashed that great big smile. "I love you too, Mom." He skipped off toward the front of the house.

She let out a long breath. It was close to nine in the morning. She wasn't exactly sure what time Hawke got off work this morning, but he should be home by now. Reading one letter shouldn't take very long, and it would only take one letter for him to figure out he was a father.

"Mom! Mom! It's Dad! We found Daddy!"

Hawke hated it when people showed up at his house unannounced, so he decided to call Calista first, but she let it go to voicemail. He glanced over his shoulder. Duncan remained in the passenger seat of the truck with the window rolled down. He pulled his ball cap over his head, and Hawke suspected Duncan was about to take a little snooze.

He raised his hand three times before his finger finally connected with the doorbell. Not wanting to seem too impatient, he turned his back to the door and stared at the school bus rolling to a stop down the street. He squinted, looking for his kid.

His kid.

He couldn't put words to how he felt about being a father. Surreal didn't do it justice. Maybe it was because he hadn't met him yet.

Butterflies filled his stomach as the door rattled.

"Can I help you?" a squeaky voice asked.

Hawke turned. He had to lower his gaze. Standing before him was a pint-size version of himself.

"Dad?" the boy whispered.

"Huh?"

"Mom! Mom! It's Dad! We found Daddy!" The kid jumped at Hawke, wrapping his arms and legs around Hawke's body so tight that he couldn't catch a breath.

He stumbled backward, lifting the boy higher.

He closed his eyes, pressing his cheek against the boy's head. Tears formed in the corners of his eyes.

"Your name is Wilson, right?"

"Yes! After you." Wilson snuggled his face into the side of Hawke's neck.

His legs wobbled, so he sat on the steps, blinking. A couple of tears rolled down his cheeks. Through the blinding sun, Hawke stared at Duncan, who had snatched his hat from his head and sat up taller, shock registering on his face.

"How do you know who I am?"

"Mom keeps a picture of you on the fridge, and she's told me all about you."

"She has?"

Wilson lifted his head and nodded wildly. "We were just talking about you over breakfast. We've been trying to find you, but she said the Air Force doesn't keep records of people who leave. We even looked on Twitter and Facebook and Googled you. Nothing."

"Well, I'm not on social media, and my real name isn't Hawke."

"It's not?" Wilson's sky-blue eyes went wide. "Does Mom know that?"

Hawke laughed. It had been the best-kept secret his entire life. When he'd been about the same age as Wilson, he'd been given the nickname Hawke by his older brother because Hawke had always had the eyes of a hawk. He liked it so much that shortly after, he begged his parents to stop calling him by his given name. As time went on, he dropped it. Only, he never changed it legally. His driver's license, social security card, and paycheck all said something else.

But still, very few people knew. Or dared to comment on it.

"I stopped going by it before I met your mom, but she knows it." Hawke adjusted his son, so he was on his right knee. He wanted to soak in the kid's face and memorize every crinkle and expression.

"You were in the seventh grade, and some boy was picking on Mom. You punched him right on the nose." Wilson raised his little hand, fisting and smacking it into his other hand.

"She told you that, huh?"

"Mom's told me lots of things about you, but not that you had a different first name." Wilson's smile quickly turned into a frown. "Where have you been? Mom has been searching for you."

"After I left the Air Force, I came here. I'm not sure why the letters didn't catch me until now."

Hawke didn't think he should say anything else on the subject. "Where's your mom?"

"Right behind you." Calista's sweet voice tickled his eardrums like palm trees in the breeze. "You hate your real name. It's why I never mentioned it." Leave it to her to get fixated on that.

"Yeah. What is it? My full name is Wilson Hawke Alba. Mom's is—"

"Calista Nights Alba. Nights because she slept all day and was awake all night. And Calista was her mother's maiden name." Hawke turned his attention back to Wilson as anger and resentment rolled across his skin from his toes to his head. She said she hadn't kept his son from him, but that is exactly what she'd done. But now was not the time to confront her.

And never in front of the boy.

"If Hawke isn't your real name, then what is?" Wilson asked.

"If I tell you, you have to promise me never to tell people. My friends at work know, but they'd never dare use it. No one does." He pointed to Duncan, still sitting in the front of the truck. "That guy once thought it would be funny to start calling me that because he didn't like that my name was cooler than his. Then he started doing it to our friend Buddy."

"Who's Buddy?" Wilson asked.

"Another guy I work with. His parents gave him that nickname when he was born because he was named after his father, and they didn't want people calling him Junior." Hawke chuckled. "Duncan over there can be a bit of a jokester. It's all in good fun."

"I can meet the people you work with?"

"Of course." Hawke nodded, shocked at how at ease he felt with a kid on his knee, like it was an everyday occurrence.

"So, what's your real first name?" Wilson asked.

Calista sat on the stoop. "Oh, he almost never tells anyone unless he's forced to give his driver's license." She laughed. "I always thought you were going to change that."

Immediately, Hawke tensed and shifted a few inches away. "Never got around to it."

Calista's smile faded, and Wilson cocked his head, giving Hawke a puzzled expression.

"All right, Wilson, but you can't laugh." Hawke did his best to relax. His son didn't need to be dragged into a past that only brought pain and misery. "The name my parents gave me when I was born is David Donald Wilson. At one point, I was called Double D."

Wilson burst out laughing. "That's a bra size!"

"Tell me something I don't know." Out of the mouths of babes. "I haven't been called that since I was ten."

"I'm almost ten." Wilson puffed out his chest. "Mom said when we found you, that if you wanted, I could change my last name to Wilson, but that would be weird to be Wilson Wilson." The boy rolled his eyes. "But maybe we could change it to David Hawke Wilson." He nodded his head. "Yeah. That has a nice ring to it. I like it. And you changed your name and it stuck. So, I could do the same."

The air in Hawke's lungs escaped, and he couldn't suck in a deep enough breath.

"Will you all call me David from now on?" the boy asked, his excitement laced with every syllable.

"Perhaps. But right now, you're late for school. So go back inside, brush those teeth, and get your backpack."

"Mommmm," Wilson—David—whined. "I've waited my whole life to meet my dad and—"

"I think you should do as you're told. I don't live far from here, so we'll have plenty of time to get to know each other."

"You mean it?" Wilson—or maybe now David —jumped to his feet.

"Let me talk to your mom, and we can make some plans to go fishing this weekend or something."

"I love fishing!"

"Me too. Now go do as your mother said."

"Yes, sir!" David raced up the steps, nearly tripping over his own feet.

Hawke stood at the bottom of the porch with his hands on his hips, staring at the screen door as it slammed shut. "He missed the bus."

"I'll drive him," Calista said.

"I want to do that," he said behind a clenched jaw. "I want to pick him up tonight and take him to dinner. As a matter of fact, I want to spend as much time as I can with him. I'm off all week, and this weekend I have no plans."

"We don't have much going on this weekend, so we can make some arrangements. He has soccer practice on Wednesday and a doctor appointment on Thursday."

"I can take him." The longer he stood in her front yard, staring at her, the more his blood heated.

"Let's start with dinner tonight and go from there." She took a hunk of her hair and pushed it behind her shoulder. "I won't keep you from your son, but we do need to—"

"You've kept him from me for almost ten years."

She opened her mouth and let out a gasp. "How dare you? I did no such thing."

"Really? Because in one of your letters, you specifically stated you didn't tell my brother, yet you spoke to him. Sent him the letters but chose *not* to tell him about David."

"His name is still Wilson and I didn't think—"

"If he wants to be called David, then that's what I will call him. And I want to give him my last name. He deserves that. Also, you could have told Colt about David when I didn't answer your letters. He would have delivered the message to me, and I would have come running."

"Once again, my son's name is Wilson." Calista's blue eyes turned ice-cold. Much like the day he walked out of her life. "Because you didn't respond, I assumed you didn't want him or want—"

"Why wouldn't I—"

"Don't interrupt me when I'm answering your question. I tried to tell your brother, but he said whatever was in the letters was between us. He didn't want to know, nor did he want to get involved. Besides, I only saw your brother once.

Only spoke to him twice and the second time, he all but hung up on me, stating you made your position clear, but if I wanted to keep sending letters, he'd keep delivering them. I assumed you didn't…" She glanced over her shoulder. "…want him."

"You know what they say about making assumptions."

"All you had to do was open one damn letter. But you didn't care enough about me to do that." She shoved her hands into the pockets of her jean shorts. Her tanned, muscular thighs flexed as she shifted her stance. "He goes to School 18 on—"

"I know where it is."

"As long as the bell hasn't rung, you can just drop him off at the side door in the circle. You'll see a line of cars. Do you want to pick him up?"

"I would. Thank you." He swallowed the shame that smacked his tonsils with a sour taste. She was right. He should have opened the letters. Had he taken his head out of his ass, he might not have lost ten years.

But he was too stubborn and wanted to blame her a bit longer. It was easier to stay mad at her since that's the only emotion he allowed himself when it came to the woman he had once loved.

Oh, fuck. He had always loved her, but admitting that didn't change anything.

"I'll call the school. You'll need to bring your ID, and pickup is at four, right after the buses leave the loop."

"Does he have any allergies or anything I should know about?" He would have known that if he had been a better father.

A better man.

"Just don't let him eat a ton of junk, and I'd like to know where you plan on taking him."

"I'll text you the itinerary."

"I want him home by nine. He's really easygoing, and he's been dreaming about this moment his entire life. I doubt he'll give you a hard time about anything. But if you have any problems, I'll be around," she said. "And we need to have a conversation about how visitation will go moving forward. We should probably put it in writing. Of course, you'd need to actually read the documents when we—"

He raised his hand. "Okay. I deserved that. But I want to be in his life. I want to be his father."

"You are his father."

4

"Wilson—"

"I want to be called David," Wilson said. "I know what my mom thinks about all that. But don't you think it should be my decision?" He tugged at Hawke's shirt.

Hawke leaned closer.

"Like it was yours."

"All right. David, this is my buddy, Duncan." Hawke pulled open the driver's side rear door to his pickup. Screw what his given name was; if the boy wanted to be called David, then so be it. Calista was going to have to deal with it, much like his parents had when he decided Hawke was a much better name than David.

"Are you a firefighter too? Did you know my

dad when he was in the Air Force?" David hopped up into the back seat with gusto, his little body bouncing up and down with excitement as he tugged at the seat belt.

Hawke's breath stuck in his throat.

He had a son. A concept he still couldn't fathom, even though his son was the spitting image of him.

"Yes to both questions," Duncan said. "I also knew your mom, though not well."

"Wow. That's so cool," David said.

Hawke laughed. "He's not as cool as me. He's just a firefighter. I'm also a paramedic. I get to drive the ambulance. Duncan here rides in the back of the fire engine."

"That's cool too," David said. "Do you think I could get a ride in both someday?" David's big, thick lashes fluttered over his bright-blue eyes like butterfly wings. So innocent and full of life.

Hawke couldn't believe that the boy acted like they'd been old friends who just hadn't had the chance to talk in years, while he, on the other hand, had no idea how to act or even what to say. "I think we can arrange that."

"Oh. Oh. Oh. And we're having a sort of show and tell about our parents and their jobs. Mom comes in every year at whatever school I'm at, but maybe this year you could come and present to my class?"

"I'd be honored." Hawke glanced toward the house.

Calista stood on the front porch, leaning against the railing. One arm tucked across her midsection, the other held a mug. She brought the mug to her pink lips and blew before taking a sip. She waved with a slight smile.

You are his father.

The words still splashed about in his brain. She'd said them with authority. It was as if she been waiting all these years for him to show up. He had to give Calista credit. It couldn't be easy for her to let her son go off with a stranger—no, he wasn't a stranger.

He was a father.

But still. She didn't have to let him have all this time with David. She could have been a bitch and told him no. While the Calista he remembered might have had a tough exterior, her heart was as soft as a puffy white cloud.

"But let's check with your mom first. She might have her heart set on coming to speak to your friends."

"Oh. Yeah. That's a good idea," David agreed as he raised his hand to his face, rubbing his chin. "Mom would be hurt since I already asked her to do it."

"We don't want to hurt your mom, so maybe next year." Hawke slammed the gearshift into reverse and eased out of the driveway, heading north. The school was only a ten-minute drive, but Hawke drove a few miles slower than usual, wanting to soak in every second he could with his son. He loved the way his little voice tickled his ears. In an instant, the boy made Hawke want to be a better man. A happier man.

A whole man.

The butterflies in his stomach turned to rocks dropping heavy in his gut. He walked through the last ten years without even experiencing a single thing. Sure, he'd accomplished a lot in his career, but that's all he had.

He thought it had been enough until he opened that first letter. Gripping the steering wheel, he pulled into the school's circle, following the line of cars dropping off students.

"I've got an idea," Duncan said. "We could set it up with the school for our entire team to come on a separate day. We've done that with Arthur's kids, our boss."

"You could really do that?"

"We sure could," Hawke said. "That way we won't take anything away from your mom."

"With the fire engine and the ambulance?" David leaned over the center console. "Could we go for rides?"

"We can't take the entire school, but maybe we could take just your class," Duncan said. "We've done that before for other family members on our team."

"Do you have kids?" David asked with wide eyes.

"I've got a little girl and a baby boy, but they are too young yet to be interested in firefighting," Duncan said.

"This is going to be great, Dad! I can't wait to see the expression on Blaine's face when he doesn't get to go for a ride."

"Who's Blaine?" Hawke asked. Who the hell named their kid Blaine?

"He's this jerk who thinks he's better than everyone else. His dad's a cop, and his class got to go to the police station for a special tour and ride in the cop cars and he's even been on the back of a motorcycle. One time last year, they brought the K9 Unit. I didn't live here then, but it did sound cool. I told Blaine all about you. Thing is, he doesn't believe my father was in the Air Force or is a fire-fighter. He thinks I'm lying."

"Well, you're not. And you'll get the chance to prove it." Hawke's heart expanded in his chest. He remembered being a little boy, about David's age, when his own father came to school to talk about being a cop. He thought his dad had been the most incredible dad there until stupid little Jimmy Reed's dad showed up in his SWAT vehicle. And not just one. He brought the entire team. No one cared about what his father did anymore.

Hawke had been devastated because Jimmy's dad happened to pull into the school right in the middle of his father's presentation. His father hadn't cared at all. He said bravado would always be a man's downfall.

"Be humble, son. Knowing in your heart that what you do is important and matters more than what others might think. And showing off, well, that is a sure sign of a man who doesn't understand his own worth."

His father's words might be true, and they served him well as an adult.

But the little boy needed to show off.

"I better go before the bell rings." David wrapped his arms around Hawke and kissed his cheek. "See you after school."

"Later, little man." Hawke reached around to ruffle the boy's hair, but instead, he gave him a long hug. "Be good."

"It was nice meeting you, Duncan," the boy said.

"My pleasure, dude." Duncan gave David a fist bump.

"Oh, no. That's Blaine," David said as he slipped from the cab of the truck.

Hawke, well aware he had on his fireman's shirt, stepped from his pickup and rounded the hood. A young boy, dressed like he should be a mannequin in the front of some hipster store, stood on the sidewalk with his hands looped into his backpack straps. His blond hair was perfectly styled like the male models you see on billboards.

Hawke stood next to David, resting his hand on the boy's shoulder.

David glanced up and covered his mouth with his hand. "I should probably tell you that Blaine's parents are divorced, and his father has been trying to get Mom to go out to dinner ever since we moved here. I don't think Mom likes him, but Blaine's dad doesn't seem to care."

Hawke tried not to clench his fist, but it proved impossible.

"Hey. You're holding up the line," a man yelled from the shiny BMW that Blaine had stepped from. One more car was parked behind the BMW.

"Sorry. I haven't seen my son in a while, and I just wanted to give him a proper goodbye. I'll be out of your way in a second." He took David by the shoulders and smiled. "That should take care of what Blaine thinks."

"You're Wilson's father?" the same man asked as he made his way across the pavement. "We thought *he* was missing in action, or just plain missing from his kid's life in general."

Yeah, that last statement was just about right, something he wouldn't ever let happen again. "I'm alive and well, thank you. And my son wants to be called David from now on." Hawke stared at the man.

Fucking Wendel.

"I'll try to remember that. I'm Wendel Lawrence."

Of all the people in the world, he had to come face-to-face with this asshole. "I know who you are." Hawke glanced at David, who stuck out his chest proudly.

Wendel looked him up and down, as if trying to place him. As if he didn't know. Jerk. "I do believe we might have crossed paths. I'm a local police officer and ex-fighter pilot for the Air Force."

"Can't say I ever heard of you when I was in the Air Force." He tapped his chest. "I'm a paramedic and firefighter here locally. I was at your house six months ago when—"

"I'd rather not discuss that in front of the children," Wendel said with a hushed tone.

David stared at him with wide eyes and a beaming smile.

"You best be on your way in, son," Hawke said, much like his own father would have. "I'll see you after school." He gave David's hair a good ruffle.

"Bye, Dad!" David took off running for the front door.

"Don't you dare ever bring that up in front of those kids. It's a bogus allegation that doesn't even deserve my department's attention. I'm the one who stepped back because it's the right thing to do until all this is cleared. My son has no idea about the allegations, and I'd like to keep it that way because soon, it will disappear."

Hawke raised his hands. "I wasn't talking about that, but the fire, which is problematic at best. There's a reason my department hasn't closed that case." Hawke folded his hands across his chest.

Nothing like a good pissing contest.

"Something else that doesn't need to be discussed in front of my son," Wendel said. "What I'd like to know is where on earth have you been for the last ten years? My son tells me that your boy hasn't even met you, until now. That's some real good parenting there."

"What I've been doing is none of your business."

"How is Calista?" Wendel asked. "What a fine woman, that one." He brought his index finger and thumb to his lips and made a smacking noise. "Beautiful. Smart. I like her a lot. We went out once and I'm looking forward to taking her out again."

Hawke clenched his hands into tight balls. If he wasn't in a school parking lot, he'd not think twice about punching this guy right between the eyes. "Stay the fuck away from my son and Calista."

"Or what?" Wendel asked. "Last I looked, Calista was single and free to be with any man she wanted, including me."

"That's not happening," Hawke said. "I better not see you hanging around her or my kid."

"Is that a threat?" Wendel asked. "Because if it is, I'll have my buddies—"

"No threat. And you're not a cop right now." Hawke shook his head. "But I will warn you that if you go anywhere near Calista, or my son, it won't be Kaelie and her investigation you have to worry about."

Wendel inched closer, their noses only a few inches from each other. "Kaelie needs to resign. She's botched up too many investigations. It has gotten in the way of good police work. No woman, especially a pregnant woman with two other children at home, should be doing that job."

Kaelie and Chastity took a lot of shit as working mothers and even more because they were first responders. They were both more qualified than most. Their gender or the fact they had children shouldn't even be part of the conversation.

"And you tell that boss of yours, Arthur, yeah, I know him. Ran into him a few times in the Air Force a long time ago, that I want the arson report filed. I've waited too long. He's stalling and there is no reason for it." Wendel poked Hawke in the shoulder.

He glanced down, taking in a deep breath. "Touch me again and I'll deck you."

"Go ahead. I dare you." Wendel had the nerve to give him a little shove. "Hit a cop and see what happens. Being a first responder doesn't give you immunity."

"Asshole," Hawke muttered, cocking his fist.

"Don't do it," Duncan called from the truck. "Trust me, that prick's not worth it."

Wendel glanced over his shoulder. "Well, well. If it isn't Duncan Booker. How's that child bride of yours?"

"More woman than you'll ever be a man," Duncan said with venom in his tone.

Hawke shook out his hand. He had a tendency to use his fists instead of his mouth, and it got him in trouble more than once. "I'm walking away. Remember what I said."

"You're a pussy," Wendel said. "Not man enough for a woman like Calista."

"That's it." Hawke drew back his right arm and punched Wendel in the gut.

He doubled over laughing. "You hit like a girl."

"Get in the truck," Duncan yelled.

"You're lucky my buddy was here to stop me from beating the shit out of you, because that's what I really want to do." Hawke jogged around the car, climbed in, and punched the gas.

"Kaelie's not going to like you getting in his face like that. This case is hot enough as it is," Duncan said. "He's a decorated police officer. He has some metals from the Air Force, though his record isn't that glowing. Those medals came out of combat, and while he deserved them, he was a hothead. Before you joined our team, we had a run-in with him on a mission. He's cocky and his CO had written him up more than once. Rusty says he's an arrogant fuck and hates working with him. But you didn't need to haul off and hit him. Kaelie's going to have your head on a platter for that one. So is Arthur and Rex."

"And if that man had hit on Chastity or his kid was giving yours a hard time, what would you do?"

"I might have hit him," Duncan said with a smile. "I've always known you were wired a little different than the rest of us, and that's what we love about you, but you do have a wicked temper," Duncan said. "I get you're upset about Wendel. The guy's a jerk and if the rumor mill is true, then he's a criminal too. But we don't need anyone slapping the cuffs on you."

"Wouldn't be the first time I spent the night in

county lockup." Hawk pounded the steering wheel. "That man is accused of raping women. I'm not letting him near my son and I certainly don't want him trying to seduce Calista."

"I wouldn't either," Duncan agreed. "I have to ask. That boy of yours certainly bonded with you real quick. How on earth did that happen?"

"I'm not totally sure about everything, but I think she's been telling him I didn't know he existed and she was searching for me all these years."

"That's either the cruelest thing anyone has ever done or the most genius, because that kid already idolizes you. Now, if I could get my little girl to feel the same way about me. It's all, mommy this and mommy that. Mommy's the best. And Mommy doesn't even fight fires anymore, but she's sooooo much better than Daddy. When she was an infant, she would light up like a Christmas tree when I walked in the room. She turned fifteen months, and we had a little boy, and everything is different. It's like daddy's so boring."

Hawke burst out laughing. "You've got an infant boy at home to make into a little mini Duncan and he'll follow you around like a lost puppy."

"He's only eight weeks old, but he's already showing signs he prefers mommy. I mean, he's stuck to her breast and won't even let me give him a bottle."

"You're pathetic. Besides, isn't your daughter the one who can't go to sleep unless she says good night to daddy?"

Duncan shrugged. "I do give the best butterfly kisses."

"This is a conversation I never thought I'd have." He chuckled. "With anyone."

Duncan's hand came down on Hawke's shoulder. "You're taking all this quite well. Maybe a little too well?"

"I don't think any of it has sunk in. It's like I'm living in some crazy alternate universe. I'm waiting for someone to unplug me and tell me it's all fake." Hawke spent a lot of time with the men on his team while he was at the station. The ones who were married, he met their wives and all their children. While he avoided close emotional contact, he still considered them family.

He enjoyed experiencing these men's bonds from a safe distance. He'd never been jealous of their tight friendships. He admired and respected them.

He didn't want it for himself until now, but he

wasn't sure how to ask for it. "Do you know that tattoo place near the fire station?" Hawke asked.

"I have an appointment there in an hour. I'm adding my son's name and birthdate to the heart I did when Laurie Ann was born."

"Aw, that's cute," Hawke said. "Let's go now. I want to add a couple of words to the one on my back."

"Isn't that the same tattoo you brother's buddy, Peter, has?"

"I changed it up a bit, but now that I have a kid, I need to add to it."

"And what are you planning to add?" Duncan asked.

"I want it to read:

I will honor my brothers-in-arms along with their loved ones.

Freedom isn't free and I will defend it with my life.

It is the quiet professional that rules the day.

And family rules the heart."

"Family is everything," Duncan said. "And you're as much a brother to me as my own flesh and blood. You aren't in this alone."

"Yeah. I know. That's why you're going to stick up for me when Arthur, Rex, and Kaelie find out I punched Wendel."

"I heard the entire exchange, and Wendel kind of deserved it. I've got your six."

"Thanks, man. Now, let's go get some ink." A little physical pain might give him a chance to clear his mind and figure out a way to deal with his emotions.

And Calista.

Calista sprinted down the hallway of the school toward the principal's office. It wasn't the first time her son had been in a fight, but it was the first time he'd been the one to do the punching.

"Wait up."

She skidded to a stop and nearly fell over when she saw Hawke jogging in her direction. "What the hell are you doing here?"

"The school called me too."

"Why did they do that?" She brushed her hair from her face and let out a long breath. "Oh. I added you as an emergency contact and also listed you as his father."

"You did?"

She nodded. "I hope that's okay. You said you

wanted to be part of his life, and well, I thought since, um, well…"

His strong fingers curled around her biceps, and he tugged her closer. "Thank you."

"For what?"

"My last words to you ten years ago were *I'm dead to you*. Thanks for keeping me alive in his eyes. You didn't have to do that."

She covered her mouth, doing her best to keep Niagara Falls from taking off all her mascara and smudging it down her cheeks. "You were never dead to me. Or him. Not even when he asked me if it was possible you died in action or in a fire and trust me, I thought about telling him that every year."

"You're a good woman and a great mom. Now let's go find out what *our* son did and why. But for the record, if he stood up for someone's honor, he's *my* kid. If it's something else, he's *yours*."

"Spoken like a true dad." She swiped the tears away and stiffened her spine. No one would ever look at her with pity in their eyes again. Her son had a father who genuinely cared about Wilson's— David's well-being. That's all she ever wanted.

"I might not have acted like one earlier," Hawke said.

She glanced up at him with narrowed eyes.

He bit back a smile. That had always been her go-to disappointed look.

"What does that mean?" she asked with a tilt of her head.

"Once we bail our kid out and he's out of earshot, I'll fill you in. I just hope it wasn't my actions that brought us here."

Our kid.

That sounded and felt like she'd been tossed from a roller-coaster ride into deep space. Now, she floated above the Earth, looking down at the tiny dot and wondering how the hell she'd gotten there in the first place.

Of all the ways she imagined this going over the years, this wasn't how she'd fantasized about it. She'd wanted to believe he'd make for a great dad. But as the years passed and he didn't write, call, or show up, she figured if Hawke ever did meet his son, it would be awkward, clunky, and only out of obligation.

"I don't like the sound of that." She rounded the corner and stepped into the principal's office, Hawke one pace behind. "What did you do?"

"Let's just say some things about me haven't changed."

"Good grief," she mumbled.

"Ms. Alba," the principal greeted her with an outstretched arm. "And you must be Mr. Wilson."

"I am." Hawke shook the man's hand. He stood tall, proud, and confident. "But please, call me Hawke."

Her stomach flipped around like a fish out of water. "Where's my son?"

"He's in my office. I wanted to talk to you for a minute alone."

"What happened?" Hawke rested his hands on his hips. His biceps bulged through the thin fabric of his shirt. "All I was told was that David got into a fistfight."

"Fistfight? All you said was he and another boy got into a fight," Calista said, keeping her frustration in check. It wouldn't do her any good to fly off the handle.

"I apologize if I didn't make that clear. It started when he told everyone he wanted to be called David, because that's his father's full first name."

"David is my given name. When I was his age, my family teased me about having hawklike vision. It stuck. No one has called me David since. His name might be Wilson, my last name, but the boy would like to share in that now. So if he wants to be called David, I don't see the problem. We will change it legally anyway when we change his last name."

Calista swallowed her initial reaction. This wasn't the time or place to get into all of that. And the principal didn't need to hear it. But Hawke had gone and said it anyway. Nothing she could do about that but have a conversation with him about it later.

"It's not a problem, I assure you," the principal said. "I first want to tell you both that Wilson—I mean David—is a fine young man, so this little altercation shocked me," the principal said. "Until I heard what a few other children had to say."

"I don't mean to be rude, but could you please tell us what happened?" Calista asked.

The principal nodded. "David spent most of the day discussing how you'd finally tracked down his father. To be fair, you know as well as I do some of the children and their parents think that David has been making up stories about his father."

Calista pursed her lips. "A few of the parents have made that very clear, and as I told you—"

The principal raised his hand. "From the moment we met, Ms. Alba, I understood the situation. You made it clear that David had never met his father and that you had lost contact with him before David was born but were still searching for him. I have never once doubted or thought David was making anything up, and I've done what I can to squelch those rumors, but I have very little control over what goes on outside of these buildings. That said, I think you should know the other boy involved has been suspended for a week."

"What about David? Will he be suspended?" she asked, mindlessly taking hold of the nearest object.

Which happened to be Hawke's hand.

She half expected him to yank it away, but he clasped his firm fingers around her skin, wrapping it in comfort and warmth like a fleece blanket on a cool fall evening.

"No. But he will spend a few days in my office as punishment."

"You still haven't told us what happened," Hawke interjected. "And I'd really like to know so we, as parents, can deal with it accordingly."

"After lunch, Blaine Lawrence accused David of hiring someone to play his dad. David did what he always does and shrugged it off," the principal said.

"He's never been one to let that kind of stuff

bother him," she said. "But Blaine hasn't been very nice to my son. We've had this conversation before and honestly, I'm tired of it. My son has only been in this school for two weeks and Blaine has constantly been picking on him."

"Well, unfortunately, Blaine started calling you names, Ms. Alba, which escalated things quickly."

"Me?" She glanced up at Hawke, who hadn't said a single word in a while, but had started to squeeze her hand so hard it hurt. "What kind of names?" she asked, almost wishing she hadn't. Not only did Hawke have a short fuse, but he could never tolerate anyone disrespecting another human, especially women.

What would he do when it came from a child?

"This is difficult for me even to say, especially when it came out of the mouth of a ten-year-old." The principal's forehead crinkled. "He said that you were his father's whore. That you took money for sex acts from other fathers at the school. He told David he had pictures to prove it."

"Jesus," Hawke mumbled. "Did Blaine have any pictures?"

"What?" She yanked her arm, but he didn't let go. "Why would you even ask such a question."

"I don't mean of you. I just mean any naughty

112

pictures at all." Hawke arched a brow. "That he could try to pass off as you. He might be a small boy, but having been ten once, and curious about such things, it's possible he had something on his phone to share with other boys, if to do nothing other than show off."

"They are in the fourth grade. Where the hell would they get pictures like that?" she asked, glaring.

"I got them from my older brother when I was that age." Hawke rubbed the side of his face.

"We took his phone after we broke up the fight, but before we could make him show us the images on his phone, his father came in, and legally, we don't have the right to force them to give us access, which his father reminded us of," the principal said. "This isn't the first time Blaine has said something like this to another child at school. He's accused many mothers of being with his father. This is Blaine's third fistfight this year, which is why we have suspended him, not something that happens often in elementary school. Actually, this is my first time having to do it. Lucky for David, he didn't throw the first punch," the principal said.

"Why is that lucky?" Hawke released her hand,

flexing his fingers before folding his arms across his broad chest.

"Because all David really did was defend himself after Blaine hit him four times, according to one of the other students."

"How did a boy manage to hit my kid that many times before someone intervened?" Hawke asked with a surprisingly calm voice. This wasn't the man she remembered. The man she knew would have punched a hole in the wall.

The only time he could ever manage to keep his temper in check was when he had to deal with Courtney, only he'd always lose his shit after the fact.

Calista's heart rate sped up as she watched and listened to Hawke handle the situation like a seasoned pro. She, on the other hand, was on the verge of losing her cool. She wanted to talk to David and hear his side of the story. Of course, she'd tell David he screwed up, though secretly she wished he hadn't waited so long to punch back. She was tired of Blaine and his father. She'd barely lived here a month, and that family had become a thorn in her side.

"It happened on the playground around the side of the school. My staff was attending to a young girl who fell off the monkey bars and had the wind knocked out of her." The principal held up his hand. "I know that's no excuse for what happened, but as soon as they saw the boys fighting, they broke it up." The principal's lips curved upward. "But not until David managed to land one right here." He pointed to his nose. "He didn't break Blaine's nose, but the blood might have ruined his very expensive shirt, which probably cost more than this fancy Target suit I'm wearing."

Calista took in a deep breath and let it out slowly, grateful for the way the principal dealt with the situation.

"We do have a no tolerance policy at the school. That is why Wil—I mean David will have in-school detention."

"I have no issue with that," she said. "I'd like to see my son now."

The principal nodded. "I think it would be a good idea to just take him home. There is only an hour left of school. I'll go get him."

Hawke leaned closer. His hot breath tickled her skin. "Sounds like he's got my left jab, but I'm going to have to talk to him about letting someone hit him that many times before defending himself."

"He's got a lot of things from you," she said

with a smile. "But I can't condone fighting, and you will do no such thing."

"You can condone defending his mother's honor and defending himself. He waited until the idiot hit him more than once. I wouldn't have waited that long."

"No. You would have thrown the first punch," she said, letting out a small laugh.

"Just like I did this morning."

"You did what?" she asked, not looking amused.

"Wendel got into my face. He said crap about you and about two of my female co-workers. One who happens to be Duncan's wife. The other is married to Buddy."

"Wow. Didn't know either one of those guys got married."

"The entire team is married. All with kids. Well, Garth's wife is due next month with their first, but that's not the point," Hawke said. "I've had a few run-ins with Wendel and I don't like the guy. Today, he pissed me off, so I popped him one."

"Good grief," she mumbled. "I'm going to need you to stop doing stuff like that, especially around our son."

"If it makes you feel any better, that is the first punch I've thrown in about two years."

"Not really."

"Mom! Dad!" David came barreling out of the principal's office with a black eye and a fat lip. He flung himself at her, wrapping his arms around her with all his might. His little shoulders bobbed up and down as he began to cry. "I tried to do what you said, Mom, but he wouldn't stop."

"You know how I feel about fighting," she said softly, kissing his head. "Come on, let's go home. We'll talk about this there."

"Can Dad come too?"

"Sure," she said. If she was going to let him be a father, then she had to deal with the fact that he'd be spending time with them together, even if it broke her heart all over again.

5

*H*awke's phone vibrated in his back pocket. He pulled it out and stared at an email from Wendel Lawrence. The subject line read: *Medical Bills.*

He tapped the screen.

I expect you to pay for my son's doctor's visit today and his clothing. The bill is attached. It seems your boy follows you, taking potshots for no reason. But that is not the nature of this email. I just wanted to get your attention.

As one former airman to another, I'd appreciate it if you told Kaelie to return the items from my home office. On Monday, I have an appointment with the DA. I'd rather not file a complaint, but Arthur and Kaelie have left me no choice. Their incompetence in finding out who set the fire will be their downfall.

And yours, if you're not careful.

By the way, letting Calista go had to be the dumbest thing you've ever done, but don't you worry, I've taken good care of her.

I plan on doing it again.

"Like hell you have or ever will," Hawke whispered.

The sound of rubber squeaking against a hardwood floor tickled his ears.

He shoved the phone in his back pocket.

"Here."

Hawke took the beer Calista offered. He sat on the front step of her house. She lived on a dead-end street in the back of a quiet, more upscale seaside neighborhood than his. Children ran about their yards yelling and laughing. A group of teenagers sat under a big tree near the entrance of a small park.

"Where's David?" he asked.

"It's going to be so hard for me to call him David all the time. But if it makes him happy, then so be it."

"And it's going to be better when he takes my last name."

"That's jumping the gun a bit, don't you think?"

"Maybe, but if I'd known about him, I would have wanted him to have my name."

She nodded. "I just want to make sure that any decisions we make are in his best interest."

"Where is he?" Hawke asked again.

"Cleaning his room. I told him once he was done with that, then we'll see about him playing outside with the rest of the kids, but he really should have some kind of consequence, don't you think?"

"You're asking me for parenting advice?" He twisted and pulled at the paper label on his beer. "That's rich," he said sarcastically.

"I'm trying to include you in everything. I know this is overwhelming, and you're still angry."

"You don't have a freaking clue as to what I'm feeling." Nor did he. One second, he was flying high, thrilled by the strange turn of events. Minutes later, rage filled his heart. Had Calista never strapped herself to a jumper, he might not have ever known he had a kid.

Whose fault was that?

Not a question he was prepared to ponder too closely. He preferred to blame her. It made it easier, just like it had to blame both of them for Courtney's death so he could be an asshole and walk away.

"Why don't you tell me how you're feeling?"

"Why? So, you can psychoanalyze me?" He

kept his gaze on the young girl skipping rope across the street. He counted the number of times her feet hit the pavement while he continued to remove the paper label from his longneck. He wasn't sure when it happened, but somewhere along the way, he'd mastered feeling sorry for himself.

"Now you're just being an asshole because you can."

She had a point. "How long have you lived here?"

"About three weeks."

He shook his head. "I'm five miles south of here."

"It's a small world." She took a seat next to him. Leaning back on her elbow, she gulped some of her beer. She hadn't aged much over the last ten years. A few small lines around the eyes and she might have put on a few pounds, which were sorely needed, but she looked exactly as he remembered.

"I'm sorry you've had to raise him all alone. Had I known, I would have been there for you. For him."

She jerked her head back and laughed. "One minute, I'd be mad as hell at you, and I'd write you some nasty stuff. The next day, I'd be daydreaming over you meeting your son and what that reunion would be like, as well as us being a family. Kind of like how you're treating me now."

He reached out and clanked her nearly empty bottle. "I know. I read all the letters."

"I meant every single word. Even when I said I still cared and thought about you."

"That I find hard to believe after all these years," he said, slightly amused by the way her lips curved into a half smile. "I deserved your wrath."

She'd always had a light, calming effect on the people around her, no matter the situation. When he'd been with her, she believed that if you can't laugh at yourself, you shouldn't laugh at all. Her life had been one tragic event after the other, and yet she managed to remain positive.

It seemed like she continued on the positive train long after he left her standing in that cemetery.

His mother told him on her deathbed that she had no regrets, and that was the one wish she had for her boys.

He'd failed his mother the day he walked away from Calista.

And he failed his son.

Two regrets he'd spend the rest of his life trying to make up for.

"I couldn't believe the man I knew would just up and abandon his child. But that's what I was left with when you didn't answer my letters."

"I would never do—"

She pressed her palm over his mouth. "That's why I kept writing, regardless of how much you hurt me. I'd look at our son, and I knew deep down that something had to be keeping you from him. I just didn't know what. Since you'd left the Air Force, and Colt had confirmed that for me, but he wouldn't tell me anything about your life, because he'd promised you he wouldn't, all I could was write. I can't tell you how many things ran through my brain. Mostly that you'd fallen in love, gotten married, and had a bunch of kids, and one more wasn't in your game plan."

"That's just ridiculous. You know me better than that."

"I thought I did. But I kept waiting. For ten long years, I would stare at my cell and wait by the door, hoping, praying that one day you'd show up." She dropped her hand to her side. "I did it because of your son. He's certainly a chip off the old block, that's for sure."

"He told me that he waited for just the right moment to sock the little turd in the nose, just like you told him I did." Pride filled Hawke's mind, but at the same time, he was reminded of Wendel and the women who'd been raped and murdered. It had everyone on edge, simply because it meant the rapist/murderer was most likely a man who was supposed to be one of the good guys, making it harder for the community to trust any of them. They had been down this road before, one too many times, and none of them wanted to do it again. "I don't think giving him any form of punishment is the right thing to do. He had every right to defend himself."

"I actually totally agree with you. I hated even scolding him. Blaine has been nothing but mean to Wilson—David—ever since we moved here. I've tried talking to Blaine's father, but he doesn't think his kid could do anything wrong."

Hawke gripped the bottle, his knuckles turning white. "Are you interested in Wendel Lawrence? Romantically?" He had no claim to Calista, and he had no right to be even the slightest bit jealous, but Wendel was a piece of shit. "He mentioned that you have gone out on a date. Have you slept with him? Are you going to go out with him again?"

She tilted her head toward the sun, exposing the soft underside of her kissable neck. He used to spend hours dribbling her with kisses right under her earlobe. It was where she tasted like sweet coconuts.

"Are you kidding me? You think I'd honestly sleep with a man whose son is bullying mine? Are you nuts?"

Hawke shrugged. "I had to ask."

She sighed. "Wendel thinks he's charming. But he's not. I went out with him for a drink. I thought maybe it might help with the boys, but that's not what happened, and I refused his advances. I knew about his reputation, but I didn't need to hear the gossip to know he believes he's God's gift to women." She visibly shivered. "I hate men like that, and I can't believe you would ever think I would be interested in him at all."

"I haven't been around in ten years. I wouldn't know." Hawke wanted to know how his son handled the marriage, and the divorce, but one thing at a time, and there were more pressing matters to deal with. "I need you to stay away from Wendel, and I think it's a good idea if we keep David away from Blaine."

"That won't be hard to do for the next week, but after that, they are in the same school, so impossible."

"We could enroll David in Rolling Hills. It's a private school and a bit pricey, but I could swing it. Most of my team members who have kids send them there. It's supposed to be really good."

"I'm not moving my kid because of a bully." She leaned forward, clasping her fingers together around the bottle. "David knows everything that Blaine said was total bullshit. He waited to hit back because I've always told him never to throw the first punch because that's what got you into so much trouble, even when you did the honorable thing."

"Blaine's father isn't a bully. He's a bad man. It's all over the news about the fact the fire at his house wasn't an accident. I was there, and I agree. But other things are going on that I can't get into."

"He claims his ex-wife did it. I've never met her, so I have no idea what kind of person she is, but either way, Wendel makes me skittish."

"I've only met her in passing, but me and my team all know people who travel in hers and Wendel's circle. Especially Rex and his wife Tilly. They all say she's been put through the wringer with Wendel, and they are engaged in a real nasty custody battle," Hawke said.

"Divorce can make people crazy."

"Tell me something I don't know," Hawke said.

"I don't know how much I can tell you, which is why I asked my boss and the investigator for the fire department to stop by."

"Here? Now?"

"Arthur is bringing his wife, kids, and chicken wings. Kaelie, the investigator, is bringing her husband Buddy. You remember him, right?"

"How could I forget that one." She fanned her face. "So cute and sweet too."

"And here I thought you had the hots for the Jolly Green Giant."

"Oh, he was adorable, too, with the way he always tumbled over his words every time he got near a good-looking woman." She laughed.

Hawke shook his head. "Well, Buddy and Kaelie are bringing their twins, along with some corn on the cob, bread, and dessert. It will feel more like a gathering; Arthur's oldest boy, Justice, is almost eleven. A new friend for David. It will be fun for him, and hopefully, Kaelie and Arthur can give us some insight and fill you in on some details that aren't public knowledge."

She jumped, planted her hands on her hips, and glared. "You can't just invade my home. Call them and tell them there has been a change of plans. I don't want to entertain anyone, much less play family with your friends. You might be David's father. I will go along with this name change, but only because if and when I found you, I wanted him to have your last name and I had every intention of calling him Hawke, but I couldn't bring myself to call him that. You are his father. That is biology that can't be changed. But I'm not going to play footsie with you under the table while kids frolic in the background."

"Whoa. Wait a minute." He ran a hand across the top of his head. "I'm not asking you to play anything. I thought it would be nice for David to meet some new friends and you as well."

"I don't need new friends," she mumbled.

"Okay." He held his hands in the air as if he'd waved the white flag. "But that doesn't change the fact that something is going on with Wendel, and I wanted to present some new information to you because I don't want that man anywhere near you or David."

"And that couldn't have been done over the phone? Jesus, Hawke. You know I hate it when people make plans for me. Besides, it's too soon for us to hang out with other families. All of this is going to take time. We all need to adjust, and there will be bumps along the way. We can't just leap into the deep end. Call them and tell them not to come." She held up her phone. "Or David and I are leaving."

"Oh no, you don't." He waved his finger. "I'm the only one in the deep end, and you're the one who shoved me there. And frankly, I'm drowning. You and our son, on the other hand, have been living in a world where I was lost and needed to be found. He knew all about me and my life. How you and I met. What my favorite color is. He's been listening to stories about his father. I've had jack shit. Until today."

"And that's your fault, not mine," she said with rage dripping from each syllable like a rabid dog. "It's not like I didn't write. Send pictures. Give you updates and tell you about him. You're the one who chose to act like a fucking child, stomp your feet, and bury your head in the sand."

"Not the point," he managed behind a clenched jaw. "And the issue here isn't you, me, or David. The issue is there is an open investigation regarding Wendel, and I'm trying to keep you safe and informed while at the same time trying not to scare the shit out of our son. Besides, he wanted to meet some of the men I work with and I wanted to... to..." He rubbed his temples. "I wanted to show him off. I didn't know I could love someone so much or be so proud, and it happened in less than a day. You've had ten fucking years to be a parent. I've had hours and I'm not going to let you take this away from me."

She opened her mouth but slammed it shut when a Suburban rolled to a stop in her driveway. A young boy with dark hair jumped out of the driver's side rear door. "Hey, Hawke." The boy waved wildly. "Dad says there's actually someone here my age to hang out with, so I don't have to deal with my little brother and sister all night by myself."

"His name's David." Hawke nodded.

"I'll be inside," Calista said as she jogged up the stairs. She didn't say hello to anyone, much less let him introduce her. She could be pissed off all she wanted. He wasn't about to regret taking care of her.

And *his* son.

Kelly, Arthur's youngest, only three years old, stumbled as her older brother, Justice, set her feet on the ground. "Hawke," she yelled, flapping her arms wildly at her sides.

Hawke lowered to one knee, his hands outstretched. The little girl had stolen his heart the first time she squished his face with her chubby little hands and gave him a big kiss and told him to 'lighten up.' He'd never laughed so hard, but the toddler had a point. "You look so pretty." He scooped her up, giving her a big kiss on the cheek.

"Come on," Maren, Arthur's wife, took the little girl onto her hip, balancing a big bag of chicken wings from the local pizza shop. "Let's go find Hawke's friend and her son."

"Jaden, get out of the bushes," Arthur yelled. "Go with Mom."

"Okay, Daddy. But there are all sorts of neat bugs, and I want to collect some."

"We don't collect other people's bugs; now scoot." Arthur slapped Hawke on the back, giving him a manly hug. "How are you holding up?"

"About the only thing keeping me from going crazy is the fact that my son is the most amazing human I've ever met, but then I realize I had nothing to do with how he's turned out so far, and I go back to wanting to take my fist and put it through a tree. Or better yet, Wendel Lawrence's face." He leaned against the railing on the porch, staring out over the front yard. Buddy and Kaelie should only be about ten minutes out, based on their last text.

"You sure did a number on his gut." Arthur

raised his hand. "Or so Rusty said. I guess Wendel went to his boss and then the chief. Wendel was looking for blood, specifically yours. Since there were no witnesses that anyone was made aware of, it's your word against his, and he decided to let it go. For now."

"I barely hit him," Hawke said, shaking his head. "Let's dive in. What do you know that I don't? And what can we tell Calista?"

"We both know that fire was hinky the second we went inside. Me, Rex, and Buddy have been slowly making our way through it under Kaelie. And Rusty's asked us to go as slow as possible, especially now that he's been suspended."

"Wendel told me he voluntarily stepped down." Hawke rolled his eyes. "Because it was the right thing to do."

"I'm sure his captain wouldn't correct him, or anyone else on the police force if pressed, but that's not what happened. Originally, our investigation didn't have anything to do with the rapes, but that all changed, and that's why he's under investigation."

"That's interesting," Hawke said. Since he wasn't on the arson side of things, he wasn't privy to these discussions. "Did you and Kaelie find something in that fire?"

"Anything salvageable went to the CSI team along with a few charred items." Arthur pointed down the street. "Rusty had his own thoughts about Wendel and went to Kaelie, asking to see what we'd gathered. He believes some of those things could be tied to the rapes and murders and has asked us to slow down this process while he sorts it all out. You know how hard it is going after one of your own."

"I sure do." Hawke nodded.

Buddy's SUV slowed to a stop in front of Calista's house. Buddy worked with Arthur on the arson team, something Hawke thought about training for, but that meant it would take away from being a paramedic and he loved that just a little too much.

Kaelie stepped from the passenger side, her growing belly gaining in size every day.

A second set of twins.

Insanity.

Hawke couldn't imagine doing two at once.

Then again, he had no idea what it was like to have a baby and he'd never be given that chance.

Buddy set one of his three-year-old twins on the

ground while Kaelie handed him a screaming child. "Where are the other kids?" Buddy asked.

"Probably the backyard. Just go through the house." Hawke held open the door.

"Can I pawn these two off on Maren?" Buddy asked. "I want to be part of this conversation."

"Aww, my honey has FOMO." Kaelie raised up on her toes and kissed Buddy's cheek. "Don't worry, babe. What I tell them, you already know."

"Why don't we move this to the backyard," Hawke said as he gave Arthur a slap on the back. "I want Calista part of the conversation since this concerns her too."

"Hawke." Kaelie grabbed his biceps. "I can't tell her certain things. Not only is she not a member of the team or a police officer, but this case is about to get real hot. Too hot and if she were to repeat any of it, it could blow our chances of nailing this asshole. And I certainly don't want to have it in front of the children. Let's keep it right here, for now."

Hawke ran a hand over his growing beard. He shouldn't let it grow like this because he would have to shave it off after his forced vacation. "Break it down for me as best you can, but I will have to tell her something."

"All right." Kaelie sat in the rocking chair and rubbed her belly. "But I can't give out the details of the police investigation. Not even to you."

"Why can't you just haul his ass in?" Hawke asked.

"I wish it were that simple, but if we want these charges to stick, then we need to do this right, and that means being patient and letting Rusty work his magic. Rusty is pretty good at bringing down the bad guys."

"Easy for you to say," Hawke said, dropping his hands to his sides. "My son goes to school with Wendel's kid."

Kaelie held up her hand. "I know you punched him on the school grounds. It has no bearing on the fire investigation. But Rusty wants to clock you one."

"Bad news travels fast." Hawke couldn't help it. He cracked a grin.

"It sure does, and I'm advising you not to do it again. We don't need him to be any more antagonistic with us than he already is. What I gathered in that fire might be helpful to Rusty, who is gathering some solid evidence, but he's a slippery motherfucker."

"Does Calista fit Rusty's victimology for the

rapist?" Hawke asked, catching Kaelie's gaze. "She's in her thirties, with long dark hair—"

"We'd have to ask Rusty that question," Arthur said with his hand on Hawke's shoulder.

"Actually, I know the answer to that. Every woman that Rusty has connected to this case, that I might have connected to the fire, was about the same age as Calista," Kaelie said. "One was married. One had kids. One did not. Rusty's looking up other cases that haven't been solved in a fifty-mile radius, looking for any file that might be similar. We've also contacted the Air Force for any rapes on the base that have been unsolved while Wendel was still enlisted. Or if there were any allegations of harassment. We don't have a clear picture yet." Kaelie's voice lacked any of the conviction she usually spoke with. "I've become more involved with this only because of the fire, and Rusty needs me to stall."

"I haven't shown this to Calista yet, but I am seriously concerned about it." He snagged his phone from his back pocket and pulled up the email he'd gotten less than half an hour ago. "I take it as a threat."

Arthur held the phone in his hand before handing it to Kaelie.

"I hate this asshole," Kaelie said, handing the cell back. "I can't tell you how many men like him I've had to work with."

"Please tell me what I'm up against," Hawke said. "I need to protect my family. My son."

"You can't tell Calista." Kaelie raised her brow. "I mean it."

"I won't tell her the specifics, but I've got to give her something. It's the whole reason you all are here, and let me tell you, she wasn't overly thrilled that I invited you."

"I'm sure she wasn't thrilled about how you left her ten years ago, either." Kaelie lowered her chin.

"Excuse me?" Hawke glared at Kaelie.

"When I asked my darling husband, he tried not to tell me. But I gave him the evil eye." Kaelie lowered her chin. "I scare him sometimes."

"You frighten everyone." Hawke chuckled. "Please, continue."

"A necklace that Arthur found in the fire might have belonged to the first victim," Kaelie said. "Rusty's hands are tied since they are in the same precinct. He doesn't know who to trust, so he needs a little time to sort that out."

"A trophy?" Hawke didn't have to be a cop to

know that many serial killers kept something to remember their victims.

Sick bastard.

"It could be." Kaelie nodded. "But it's a common necklace. I even have one, so without DNA, we don't have much." She raised her hand before Hawke could even open his mouth. "The necklace and other items are being tested as we speak, but this stuff sometimes takes time, and I'm taking more than needed. I'm also going back through everything with Rusty. If we find more trophies, we got a better chance of nailing this creep."

"I've got a kid who punched that man's son and a... a..." What the hell did he call Calista?

"It's the weekend, so there's no school to worry about for two days. This team is off for an entire week, so we'll make sure eyes are on Calista and your son the entire time." Arthur nodded. "It's what family does."

"I'm going to help Rusty put that jerk off behind bars. You can count on that." Kaelie stood just as Buddy returned to the front porch.

"What did I miss?" Buddy asked, handing his wife a water bottle and beers for everyone else.

Hawke laughed. "Everything."

"Story of my life since having kids." Buddy held up his longneck. "To family."

"To family," Hawke repeated. The new words tattooed on his back burned his skin and scorched his heart.

He had a son.

Family.

It was something he never expected.

6

"*M*om! Please! I promise to be good."

Calista shot a nasty look toward Hawke, who sat at her island in the middle of *her* kitchen. He'd all but said it would be fine. He had no right to make that kind of decision without discussing it with her first.

In private.

Not in front of a room full of children jumping up and down, begging her to let David spend the night at Arthur's house.

It didn't matter that at one time she had called Arthur a friend. Or that his wife, Maren, was about the nicest woman Calista had ever met. It didn't matter that Calista wanted to get to know Maren. That she could see them being fast friends.

And their kids? Wow.

Buddy was exactly as she had remembered. And Kaelie was the perfect woman for him. Their twins, while a handful, were as sweet as sugar.

But that didn't change how she felt undermined by Hawke, who had zero experience as a father. To his credit, he asked everyone to give them a minute to discuss the situation. Now, it was time for David to leave the room.

"Let me talk to your father. Why don't you go outside and play with Justice?"

"Yes, ma'am." David slumped his shoulders.

She kissed the top of her son's head and watched as he scuffed his feet across the wood floor, his head hung low.

"Don't ever do that again." She glared at Hawke.

"Excuse me?" Hawke held his beer halfway between the counter and his lips. "Do what?"

"You told him he could go without asking me, and this is after you bulldozed me into entertaining *your* friends. I don't like being manipulated like that."

"I'll apologize for not consulting you before inviting my friends over, but you're being delusional because all I told our son was that before any decisions were made about a sleepover, he needed to discuss it with you, but if you need one more reason to continue to hate me, be my guest." He tilted the glass bottle. "For the record, I was all for him spending the night at my boss' house. I thought it might give you and me a chance to talk alone. But now, I don't want to be in the same room with you. So tell him whatever you want, and I will one hundred percent back you up." He pushed his chair back from the counter. "I'll be outside with my friends. Shall I send David in?"

"Yes, thank you." She snagged her wineglass and took a big gulp of courage. She had two choices. Say yes and be the hero. Say no and be the mean mom.

Oh, who the hell was she kidding.

Neither of those things were true. Besides, her only reason for saying no would be to piss off Hawke. What good did that do her son?

"Hey, Mom. Dad says you have a decision for me."

She patted the stool at the island. "How do you

feel about having met your father after all these years?"

"Truth?" David responded with the family standard question. She'd raised him to be honest, but she also understood that there would be times in his life when he'd rather keep his thoughts and feelings to himself, so he had the option to keep his mouth shut occasionally.

"Always," she said.

"I love it, but I don't want to hurt your feelings."

"I'm glad you're enjoying getting to know him." She reached across the counter and held her son's hand. "It's harder for him because he didn't know about you, and I want you to know he would have been here all along had we found him earlier."

"He's told me that at least five times in the last hour."

"Have I told you how proud I am of you lately?" she asked.

David nodded.

"You're making Hawke feel loved, and that's the best feeling a father could have."

"Don't you still love him, Mom?"

Out of the mouths of babes. "It's been a long time, but yes, part of me will always love your father. He's a great man, and I think he's right. You should go spend the night with your new friend."

"Really?" David jumped from the stool and turned in a circle, flapping his arms. "Thanks, Mom. Can I go tell them?"

"Of course." She watched her son race out the back door while she poured herself another glass of wine. She held up the bottle. Only half a glass left, so she filled hers to the brim. Might as well get a little numb since she'd be spending the night alone for the first time in almost ten years.

The next ten minutes was filled with David running around, collecting what he'd need for his sleepover. His excitement filled the air, and it proved impossible to stay angry, even at Hawke.

Calista knew deep down David would be just fine. He'd been starved for this kind of interaction with kids his own age. While he made friends easily, he didn't put himself out there, mostly keeping to himself, so this truly was a blessing.

"Are you okay?" Maren asked. She stood next to the back door and smiled. "I know we're a lot to take in."

"Well, back in the day, I was used to everyone on your husband's team. But it's weird to see them all grown up, with wives and kids."

"For as long as we've known Hawke, he's been a bit of a loner, always keeping us at a distance. Most of the single men on the team do the same thing, but not to the extent that Hawke has, which is strange for Arthur, since they have such a long history. So when he called for help, Arthur offered to come over with Kaelie and Buddy." Maren's smile reminded Calista of Hawke's mother before she passed. It was kind, loving, and reassuring.

"I'm sorry if I've come across like a total bitch." Calista hadn't wanted to enjoy these people, and she tried not to but failed miserably.

"You didn't. But it was obvious to us that we were unexpected guests, so I cornered Hawke, and he explained he neglected to ask you before accepting our offer to bring dinner." Maren looped her arm through Calista's and headed toward the front door. "You should know that Arthur didn't give Hawke much of an opportunity to decline."

"That does sound like Arthur. He was always known for impromptu parties up in Dover. But Hawke still should have told me." And she should have made a better effort to tell Hawke about his son.

A regret she'd carry forever.

"Perhaps. But Arthur built this team. Every

man he works with was handpicked, and while I might be the love of his life, those men are his brothers. Their bond is thicker than we can even imagine. When Arthur says he takes care of his own, that includes those people his brothers care about. You're stuck with us."

"I could think of worse things to be stuck with." Calista couldn't remember the last time she felt like she was with her people. When she married Doug, his family had been nice enough, but she'd never been invited into their inner circle.

Hawke's friends had made her feel like family years ago and then did again today.

And then there was the connection with Hawke. It might not be exactly what they used to have, but it was still spectacular.

That terrified her.

"Mom! We're ready to go," Justice called from the porch.

"You better get going," Calista said.

"We'll take good care of him." Maren pulled her in for a long hug. "I'll call you in the morning."

"Thanks." She tossed David's bag in the back of the Suburban before kissing her son goodbye. "You be on your best behavior, you hear?"

"Yes, ma'am." David wrapped his hands around her waist. "I love you, Mom."

"I love you more," she whispered.

David skipped around the Suburban to where Hawke helped put Kelly in her car seat. "Hey, Dad," David said. "Thank you."

"For what?"

"For finding us."

"Trust me, kid. No one is happier about that than me. I'm looking forward to being a better father to you."

"You're already the best!" David jumped up into the back of the Suburban. He waved frantically from the window with the biggest smile she'd ever seen.

Tears dabbed her eyes. "I need more wine." She'd probably crack open a second bottle. She didn't drink much, but tonight certainly called for it.

"Mind if I have a glass?" Hawke asked.

"Thought you couldn't stand being in the same room with me?" She jogged up the porch steps and bolted through the main door, not glancing over her shoulder once. Her heart hammered against her rib cage, rattling her teeth. Being alone with Hawke made her want to hide under a rock, but only because she didn't trust herself around him.

Better to stay mad at him than relax and enjoy his company because if she did that, she knew they could easily end up wanting to snuggle up next to him on the sofa, and that wouldn't be good for anyone.

"I was just being mean," he said.

"We've gotten good at doing that." She pulled down another red glass and handed him a fresh bottle and the corkscrew.

"I'm sorry. I just wanted to spend time with David, but at the same time, I needed to discuss Wendel with my friends." He swirled the red liquid before bringing it up to his nose and taking a big whiff. "Remember how much I used to hate this stuff?"

"It's an acquired taste." A long silence filled the room. Years of not knowing what happened to Hawke crashed down on her shoulders.

"I could get into trouble for what I'm about to tell you, but I think you should know."

"I'm not sure I want to hear this," she said.

"Kaelie thinks, and I agree, that Wendel might have raped—"

Calista gasped. The wineglass slipped from her fingers and crashed to the floor.

"That's the second time today that someone has

broken glass when I was speaking." Effortlessly, Hawke lifted her off her feet and carried her into the family room where he set her down on the sofa. "I'll clean it up and be back in a jiffy."

"Not until you explain to me what is going on." She held his biceps as tightly as she could. So tight that he stumbled forward, landing on top of her.

"Shit," he mumbled. "Are you okay?"

Feeling the weight of his body on hers brought back vivid memories of their time together. He'd always been a passionate man. Kind. Loving. And damn good in bed.

Hell, he was the best she'd ever had, and no man could ever make her feel the way he did.

"I'll be fine once you get off me," she said under her breath, but deep down, all she wanted to do was wrap her arms and legs around his body and have him just one more time.

As if that would ever be enough.

"Sorry." He arched, pulling her up with him.

She brushed her hair out of her face. "Now tell me what the hell is going on."

"I can't tell you the specifics, but Kaelie and our cop friend Rusty believe that Wendell is responsible for the rape and murder of three women in this last year."

"Does Wendel know he's a suspect? I mean he's a cop and he likes flashing that badge of his around."

"I've been given very little information. This is why I think it's imperative we move David to the school Arthur's kids go to. He'd be in class with Justice, and my buddy Rex has a daughter there just a year younger, as well as Kent's son, who is the same age, and his daughter, who is in high school. All of the school-age kids from my team go there, and a few other friends I know as well."

"Is David in danger?" Calista took in a few deep breaths while her mind processed the information.

"I don't think so, but it's you who could be." Hawke had looped his arm over Calista's shoulders. His hand gently massaged her muscles, and she reluctantly relaxed into his body.

"What a clusterfuck," she mumbled.

"I just want to keep you and our son safe. Even though his kid won't be in school for a week, why put our son through that? Will you at least go look at the school? We can arrange for David to visit with Justice."

She rubbed her aching temples. In less than twenty-four hours, her life had turned upside down. It was hard enough to deal with Hawke being back in her life, but knowing that Wendel, who gave her the creeps anyway, could be responsible for raping and killing, made her want to move back to Vermont and in with her ex-husband.

"I just uprooted mine and David's life. I'm not sure transferring schools is what's best for him." She glanced at Hawke. "He might be an easygoing kid, but what would we tell him? What would be the reason? I'm just not sure. All I want is what's best for him."

"I think this would be good for him. It's where my friends' kids are and you watched how all that went down. We present it to him together as an option for him to be with his new friends. Make it a positive thing. Just think about it for a few minutes." Hawke jumped to his feet. "I'm going to go clean up the mess in the kitchen. Want anything?"

"Yeah. More wine. Like the whole fucking bottle."

Hawke carried two plastic glasses and a bottle of wine out onto the back patio. When Courtney had killed herself, his emotions had been all over the map. He'd felt so out of control that the only thing he could do was turn them off. He'd completely shut himself down, voiding any ties to his past. They would creep into his dreams or rear their ugly faces while on the job.

But for the most part, Hawke had kept himself an empty shell of a man.

Until this morning.

Now, everything he'd tried so hard to bury stung his body like a million bees swarming on his skin. They prickled and burned and made him want to scream. Not because he didn't want his son, or even Calista, but because of everything he'd missed out on.

And he had only himself to blame.

A reality he had to take responsibility for.

He took in a deep breath through his nose and let it out slowly between his lips. "Can we start over?"

Calista glanced over her shoulder. The setting sun glistened over her dark hair, making it shine. "Look at this."

He set the wine on the table and took her cell. A picture of David and Justice on the docks at the marina holding a couple of pretty decent-sized fish filled the screen.

"I haven't ever seen him that happy," she said. "You made that happen."

"I had nothing to do with it," he said with a long sigh.

"I don't want to fight with you," she said.

"Neither do I." He settled in the lounge chair next to her but kept his gaze on the birds taking flight in the sky. "But before we get into our personal situation, I beg you to consider having David change schools. Wendel all but threatened me in an email today."

"What? Why didn't you tell me?"

"I'm telling you now," he said, understanding her frustrated tone and well aware he probably deserved it.

"I don't like to make decisions without discussing them with David, so I do like the idea of approaching him with the concept first."

"Does that mean you talked with him before you got married? And before you divorced?" He did his best not to sound condescending or spiteful, but by the way her nose crinkled, he doubted he was successful.

"If he and Doug hadn't gotten along so well, I might not have gotten married." She cocked her head. "Why are you asking me about that?"

Hawke didn't know what bothered him more. The fact that she married someone other than him, or that his son played family with a stranger. It got under his skin, and he needed answers about this part of her past.

"How did our son take the divorce? Is he still in contact with his stepfather?" Hawke gagged on the last word. It had less to do with whoever this Doug person was, and more to do with the fact that Hawke lost ten years of his son's life. He desperately wanted to let go of the rage swirling around in his gut. But he didn't know how to do that.

She shook her head. "He's reconciling with his ex-wife, and it wouldn't be fair to his kids. Besides, David has always been so focused on you that Doug often felt left out of the equation, and I wouldn't allow Doug to squelch David's natural curiosity about his father. I didn't believe that would have been fair to you. It honestly became an impossible situation for both me and Doug."

"Was David upset about moving to Florida?"

"No. He wasn't upset at all. To him, everything is an adventure and a new place to go, looking for you. However, he sometimes misses his stepsiblings. That part was tough and about the only thing I regret."

"So you don't regret marrying Doug?"

"We had some good times together, but he'd never gotten over his wife. She was as much of a ghost in our marriage as you were." She let out a long breath. "I should have just blurted out I was possibly pregnant at Courtney's funeral. It might have saved us all a ton of grief."

Hawke adamantly shook his head. "That would have been a horrible idea. You were right to wait. I only wish I hadn't dodged you that day you showed up at my brother's. I was there, you know."

"I figured," she said flatly. "Again, I shouldn't have let your brother hush me when I thought about telling him."

"And I should have read the letters," he admitted.

"We can do this all day, but it won't change the last ten years or where to go from here." She set her glass down and leaned forward, resting her hands on his knees. "I meant it when I said I would never stop you from being a father or being in our son's life on a regular basis."

He reached out and wiped away the tears that strolled down her angelic face. He'd always hated it when he made her cry. During their relationship, he'd done it way too often.

"At Courtney's funeral, I felt so guilty for loving you." He spoke the words that had tormented his heart for years. Words that squeezed the air from his lungs every time he even thought about a long-lasting relationship with the few women he'd met over the years that he liked more than most. "I walked away because when Courtney had been alive, she managed to create a wedge between us, and in death, she just made it bigger."

Calista pursed her lips like she'd always done when angry or frustrated.

He hushed her with his finger. "We can't go back and find out if my fears would have been true, but when I saw you on the ledge, it was like someone stabbed me in the heart. I couldn't breathe, and I only thought about how much I loved you." He didn't bother to wait for a reaction. He tied their mouths up like a suction cup, unwilling to let go. Their tongues twisted and turned in a frantic dance to reunite. When he told her he was dead to her, he really meant he was dead to himself.

He thought he had nothing left to give anyway. Courtney had taken it all with her when she killed herself.

Only it had been him who had destroyed everything.

He pulled her to a standing position, still kissing her mouth as if she were his last meal.

Stumbling, he led her back into the house and pressed her body against a door when he slammed it shut. Desperation controlled his every move, and he so desperately needed Calista. He needed to love her again.

To forgive her.

To be forgiven.

To make up for the last ten years.

He dropped his head to her shoulder, breathless.

There was no making up for what he'd done. "I'm sorry," he whispered, taking a step back.

"If you're sorry about kissing me, then get out. If not, don't stop."

His gaze went between her pleading eyes and her heaving chest. He was torn between beating himself up, a mantra he'd grown comfortable in, and the deep-seated desire to be with the only woman he could ever truly love.

And damn it, he still loved her.

He let out a slight chuckle as he fanned both her cheeks. "Definitely not sorry about that."

She looped her hands around his waist, slipping

them under his shirt. Her warm fingers dug into his muscles.

"I'm just not sure it's a good idea," he said.

"Neither am I." She arched a seductive brow like she used to do when she'd saunter across the bedroom half-naked.

"We can't just pick up where we left off," he said as he fumbled with the buttons on her blouse. "But we can start something new."

"We're just reminiscing. A trip down memory lane. You don't really want me anymore."

"Are you kidding me?" He pressed his body against hers, spreading her legs and lifting her feet off the ground. "Tell me that again because my body and my heart say something entirely different."

"An hour ago, you couldn't stand to be in the same room with me. Now you want to do it right here in my kitchen?"

"Yesterday you thought I didn't want my—"

She covered his mouth with her hand. "Let's not go down that circular road again."

"Agreed." Firmly, he held the back of her thighs. "Where's the bedroom?"

"Down the hall. Second door on the right, but Hawke." She cupped his face, staring deeply into his eyes, sucking the life energy from his lungs. "I want to state for the record I don't have any idea what this means, but I know for sure we don't want David to think we're back together. It wouldn't be good for him. Can you understand that?"

Slowly, Hawke made his way down the hall, contemplating her words and their meaning. This wasn't just sex, but he couldn't define it other than perhaps healing old wounds and giving them closure.

"Wherever the three of us end up, David has to be the center," she said.

"I couldn't agree more. Now, can you stop talking?" He set her on the edge of the bed, pulling her shirt down over her shoulders, revealing her tiny white lacy bra with a front clasp. He flicked it open with his fingers, exposing her perky, full breasts.

They were bigger than he remembered. He supposed that came from having a baby.

"Did you nurse our son?"

"That's a really fucking weird question to ask right now."

He knelt between her legs and cupped her, rubbing his thumbs over her hard nipples. They puckered tighter with each flick. "I might have a few more."

"Well, wait to ask them until we're done."

"You've always been so demanding in bed." He squelched the pinch of jealousy that tickled his pride. He had no right to begrudge her any man in the last ten years. He'd had his fair share of women, which brought his own shame and guilt in this moment.

But after tonight, he vowed to prove to her that he could, and would, take care of his son.

And his son's mother.

Forever.

No way would he crash and burn on this mission.

"Would you just shut up and kiss me," she whispered.

He took her nipple into his mouth, swirling his tongue over the hard nub while he managed to roll her shoulders over her hips. A wave of dizziness rolled across his body. It was as if a vortex plucked him from his current life and hurled him into a mixture of the past and the future. There was no other woman for him in the world. He knew that ten years ago but thought he could live without her.

No way could he ever walk away again.

Nor would he let her. Not now.

Not ever.

He kissed every inch of her glorious body, not letting a single speck of skin go unnoticed. He didn't stop until she squeezed her legs tight and called out his name, convulsing into his mouth. He kissed her inner thigh, then worked his way to her luscious lips. He sucked the bottom one into his mouth, nibbling on it and catching her every moan.

All he wanted to do was bury himself deep inside her, rocking with her until they both exploded with thick passion only two people who were meant to be together could share.

He'd been with a few good-looking women who by no means could be called anything but talented when it came to making love.

But no one could ever be Calista.

She curled her fingers around him, squeezing and gently stroking him like a fiddle.

Falling onto the bed on his back, he groaned, pooling her hair on top of her head. He watched her take him into her hot mouth. With the grace of a Greek goddess, she glided her lips over him, making him see double.

"Christ," he mumbled, stiffening his body, doing his best to maintain control. His breath came in short, throaty pants.

She dared to take a break and glanced up at him with a smile.

"That's enough," he commanded. "Come here." He hadn't thought that through when she climbed up on top of him. He grabbed her hips and held her steady for a long moment, staring into her eyes. "You're still the most amazing and beautiful woman I've ever laid eyes on."

Their bodies moved in unison. Each of them knew exactly what the other one needed.

Wanted.

And neither one disappointed.

He dug his heels into the mattress and raised up with a quick thrust, pulling her chest to his as he slipped his tongue into her mouth with the same passion as their bodies. They shuddered and jerked, gasping for air for long moments before he managed to roll her to the side, taking her into his arms.

He'd come home.

Or maybe she'd come home.

Either way, he was never, ever going to let her go. He ran his hands up and down her arms, just enjoying being in her presence when it hit him.

No condom.

"Shit," he mumbled. "Are you taking birth control?"

She gasped, glancing up at him. "That wasn't too smart."

"Nothing we can do about it now." And suddenly, he didn't care. Having a kid with her had turned out to be amazing.

Having another one just might be exactly what they needed.

Now he'd gone and lost his fucking mind.

7

*H*aving sex with Hawke was a mistake she could live with, had they used protection. She was pushing forty and her biological clock was past ticking. She never thought about having another child. Not even with her ex-husband. Raising Wilson… David… was all she could manage. Another child would toss her over the edge.

Waking up in Hawke's arms was a mistake she couldn't allow to happen again. For years, she imagined him coming back into her life and them becoming a postcard family. She used to dream about them taking vacations on the beach. Or maybe to the mountains, where they would sip hot chocolate and play in the snow.

That was a fantasy, and she knew it.

Didn't matter that the sex was still mind-blowing or that she still loved Hawke with every ounce of her being.

Too many hurtful things had been said, and too much time had passed.

Sure, they could form a family because they were one.

But not one where Hawke and David made her breakfast in bed on Mother's Day. No, they'd be the type of family where David would spend half his time with his father and the other half with her. Her best hope was that they would be civil enough to have holidays together.

"Arthur will be by in about twenty minutes." Hawke stepped out onto the front patio wearing the same clothes he'd worn the night before. He handed her a cup of coffee and dared to kiss her lips.

Like an idiot, she kissed him back, letting her tongue greet his with the promise of another romp in the sack.

She jerked her head back. "You should go change."

"Why?" He made himself a little too comfortable next to her, looping his arm over her shoulders as if this were an everyday occurrence.

"I don't want David to know you slept here last night."

"He's ten. He won't notice."

She took a small sip of the bitter liquid, glaring through the steam. "He's smart. He'll be the first one to point it out."

"I guess it's lucky I have an extra shirt in my truck, then." Hawke set his mug down.

Sadly, she eyed him as he walked barefoot to the driveway. Who kept extra clothes in their vehicle?

A player. That's who.

Mentally, she rolled her eyes. The Hawke she knew was anything but a player. Even if he had a series of one-night stands, she was as sure as the sky was blue that Hawke never played them and that they always knew the score.

Breathlessly, she watched him take off his shirt. She had noticed the redness around some of the words on his tattoo but not on all of them.

She knew Colt and his buddy Peter had a similar saying on his back.

"Better?" he asked with a smile.

She nodded. "Is the tattoo new?"

"I got most of it a couple of days after Court-ney's funeral, but I added the last line yesterday."

"And family rules the heart," she said softly. "I think that is the sweetest thing you've ever done."

"I was talking with the tattoo artist, and I want to put David's birthday and his full name some-where on my body."

"You're killing me here," she said.

"Why?"

"Mostly how you're honoring our son. After ten years of not hearing from you, it's not what I expected, but it's certainly what I wanted."

"I love that boy." He smiled. "I have from the moment I opened that first letter. It hit me like a ton of bricks. And when he first called me dad, I loved him more. I had no idea I could love someone this much."

"Being a parent changes you and I can't tell you how happy I am to see the two of you together. I've wished for this moment every day since the day I found out I was pregnant," she said. "But I think it's best if we don't sleep together again. I don't want to confuse David."

"Confuse him how?"

"About us," she said, gazing at the branches ruffling in the breeze. "I absolutely want to do whatever it takes to make sure you and our son maintain a special bond. I'll do whatever it takes to facilitate that, but I don't want him to get his hopes up that you and I will be a couple."

"He wants us to be a family."

"Of course he does, and that's partly why I had reservations about letting him spend the night with Justice. It's obvious how much Arthur and Maren love each other, and their kids are fantastic. They are the picture-perfect family, and all that's going to do is make David want it more."

"He's wanted more his entire life, and don't use him to avoid us."

She let out a sarcastic laugh. "You mean like how you used Courtney's death to avoid me."

"Exactly. Regardless, we need to develop a plan moving forward, and part of that plan needs to have a place for us to figure out how we really feel about each other, without dragging our son into it."

"Last night was a reconciliation of the past, pure and simple."

"Not sure how following you into the bathroom at three in the morning and bending you over the sink is pure, and this situation isn't simple."

Her cheeks heated, remembering their extensive

lovemaking. It was as if they were desperate to make up for the past.

"It was a way to forgive each other. To let go," she said.

"You can lie to me all you want, but don't lie to yourself. I know you still care about me."

Of course she did. He was the father of her child. Not a day had gone by where she hadn't thought about Hawke. Wondered what he was doing. If he was happy. Married. Had more children. Even when she hated him, she wanted the best for him. "Caring isn't the point. Caring is what will make us good co-parents, so long as we keep the past where it belongs."

"I can do that, but I want us to have a future."

For now, she would ignore his desire to have a relationship. "We need to clear the air about one more thing and it's not going to be an easy conversation."

"What's that?"

"I don't take responsibility for Courtney's death, and I can't have that hanging over our heads. I don't want it tainting our son."

"What does he believe the reason was for our breakup?" Hawke asked as he rested his mug on the table and leaned forward, catching her gaze.

She wanted to close her eyes or turn away. Staring at him would only give away her true feelings.

And fears, which she'd rather not expose to Hawke. She needed to be strong for herself and for her son. Hawke had a track record for running when things got tough. "I don't like lying to my son, so I try to stay as close to the truth as possible."

"That doesn't answer my question."

David had always been an inquisitive boy. He wasn't shy either. His outgoing personality sometimes drained her, but in the most positive way. She admired his ability to make the world smile with him even when things weren't great for him, like when he'd broken his leg and needed a cast. All the nurses loved him and told her how lucky she was to have such a wonderful little man in her life. "I told him that we lost a close friend and sometimes things like that can cause problems in relationships."

"Look. I don't think us jumping into happy family mode is a good idea either, but we're going to be spending a lot of time together, and I have a lot of unresolved feelings," Hawke said.

"Well, resolve them. I have."

His brow curved into a sarcastic arch. "Last night says otherwise."

"I haven't had sex in over a year."

"You just got divorced a few months ago."

"It was more a marriage of convenience than anything else." In the years she'd been with her ex-husband, she'd never uttered those words, even though she and Doug knew it was true. They were both lonely and wanted someone to talk to. They'd been good friends who ended up having bad sex occasionally. Doug was a good man, and she thought that would make for a lasting, loving relationship since the true love she shared with Hawke had been so easily tossed away. "I was trying to give up on you, and Doug was a kind, sweet man. But he was still in love with his ex-wife."

"Doesn't sound like that's any way to live."

"And how have you been living?"

"Most definitely worse," he said.

"How so?" she asked. Anything to keep the conversation away from them having sex or a relationship.

"Those last six months in the Air Force were brutal. We did a three-month tour in the Middle East. Arthur thought I had a death wish. It got worse when they needed volunteers to stay an extra month and I signed up. Both Arthur and Rex were pissed. It messed with Arthur's perfect plan. But I stayed and got shot." He lifted his shirt, showing off one of his scars. "When I got back, Arthur had a heart-to-heart and told me to get my shit together. He even mentioned going to see you. But instead, the Air Force let me go a month early because of my injury. Arthur sent me here to meet with the Aegis Network. They put me to work, sending me on assignments. The first few were a little boring. Bodyguard type shit. But I begged for action, and I got it. For the first few years, I was assigned most of the more dangerous missions. Anything to get my blood pumping and to feel that adrenaline in my veins. It numbed every other emotion I had so I didn't have to deal with what happened."

She swallowed the gasp that bubbled up from her gut. Never once had she thought about dying. Maybe that had been because less than a week after Courtney had killed herself, she knew about David. She always had a piece of Hawke. "All because of what Courtney did," she whispered.

He shook his head, glancing down at his feet. "No. It all had more to do with the fact I knew deep down in my soul I had made a mistake."

This time, she couldn't control the guttural response to his statement. "Are you just coming to this realization? Or is it something you've thought about from the beginning?"

"Both."

"I don't see how that's possible."

He took her hands in his, pulling her closer. "The day at the cemetery, I wanted to change my mind. I wanted to hold you and love you and cry with you."

"Why didn't you?" Hearing this now didn't make up for the last ten years of tears, but she desperately wanted to know why.

She needed to know what he was thinking and feeling at the time to make sense of everything that had happened in the last couple of days.

"I wanted to feel the kind of pain that Courtney felt."

"You wanted to feel alone?" Calista couldn't be certain exactly how or what had been going on in Courtney's mind or heart, but years of training and practicing as a therapist helped Calista understand that many of her clients felt an overwhelming and utterly consuming sense of loneliness.

"I wanted to know what it was like to be separated from the one person I loved more than anything in this world. To feel that crushing anguish in my heart."

"Do you have any idea how fucked up that sounds?"

"So says the professional." He tugged at her hands, pulling her into his lap.

Her mind told her to move back to her chair, but her heart seemed to rule her actions right now. Besides, it felt so good to be in his arms, even if it was going to end again. "And you ended up hurting me while torturing yourself."

"I am sorry for that," he said. "I seriously considered reaching out to you, but I was in the Middle East. When I got back, I was injured, and then I moved. I just kept coming up with excuses." He cupped her chin, rubbing his thumb across her cheek and neck. "I became numb, and from then on, I've kept a safe distance from everyone, including Colt. We've barely spoken over the last few years. He told me to get my head on straight and call you."

"You're making it hard for me to hate your brother." She didn't even bother to try to keep from smiling. All she'd ever wanted was the truth from Hawke. To understand his actions. It didn't matter how crazy they seemed, or even irrational, but knowing why gave her some peace.

And it would be the stepping stone to healing so they could be friends.

Which meant she really needed to get off his lap.

"When it sunk in that I had a son, with you, every emotion I've ever tried to bury, destroy, ignore, or toss away smacked me in the gut. I haven't been living for the last ten years. I've been waiting to die. I'm the first one to volunteer for every dangerous assignment. It pisses off Arthur because he then has to deal with a swing at the fire station when I'm gone. But it's also because he's watched me pull away and he's worried. He's tried to block my requests a few times, and he's made it damn near impossible for me to transfer to a different firehouse, which I've tried to do now twice. But Arthur won't let me go and I'm starting to understand why."

He spoke so fast and with such passion that she couldn't bring herself to tell him to stop, even though she knew enough to accept, forgive, and move forward.

"I've been with these men for nearly fifteen years. We were so close when were in the Air Force. But once we got here, and Arthur met and married Maren, I began pulling away. I stopped hanging out

175

with everyone outside of work. I'd find reasons not to do some of the things I loved, like hiking and fishing with the guys, because I didn't want to be around them."

"Why?" she managed to interject.

"That male bonding crap crawled in under my skin, reminding me of what I walked away from. Only Arthur likes the team he built and isn't prepared to let any of us go."

"Sounds like you've got yourself a little work family." Without thinking, she cupped his face and brushed her lips across his. "You're a good man, and I know you'll be a great father. We'll figure all this out."

"Us too?" He slipped his hands under her shirt, tenderly massaging her aching muscles. "I know we can't just pick up where we left off. We've both changed, not to mention we have a son, but we should spend time together. Date."

"You want to date me?"

He nodded with the same stupid grin he had when she finally said yes to dating him the first time, even though they had done so in secret. The only person who knew about them for the longest time had been his brother Colt, and who would he tell?

"What's the worst that can happen?"

"We hurt our son," she said, dropping her hand to her lap. She tried to stand, but he held her tight.

"No matter what happens, I'm committed to being a family. I think we owe it to our son to see if there is more than hot sex still between us." He pressed his mouth against hers while his tongue darted into her mouth, swirling around like wine hugging glass. He'd always been a master at kissing. His lips had always been soft and tender but demanding at the same time. He tasted like a warm summer breeze rolling in off the ocean.

She'd felt safe and loved whenever she had been in his arms.

This moment was no different, and that scared her.

"Do you have to do that in front of the entire neighborhood?"

Calista jumped at the sound of her son's voice. She hadn't even heard the Jeep that had stopped in her driveway only thirty feet away.

"I mean I'm happy about it, but it's kind of gross," David said.

"Trust me, it won't be gross when you're sixteen." Arthur stood next to David with his hand on his shoulder.

"You can think it's gross for as long as you like

because your mama isn't ready for you to grow up." Calista pulled her son in for a hug, giving him a big kiss on the cheek while her own cheeks heated from embarrassment.

She wasn't sure if it was from her son catching her making out with his father or from the way Hawke continued to look at her with lust—and maybe something akin to love—in his eyes. She'd seen that look many times years ago. It unnerved her then, but today it made her question every decision she'd made in the last ten years.

"Did you hear about the yacht we were invited on today?" David asked as he practically pranced on tiptoes.

"I haven't had the chance to tell your mom about that," Hawke said.

"Because you were too busy kissing." David's face scrunched up as if he'd just eaten something sour. "Can we go?"

"Most of the team and their families are going," Arthur said. "I know Rex and his wife Tilly would love it if you all came. It's a lot of fun between the yacht, Jet Skis, and they even have a power boat for tubing and such."

"Please, Mom? Can we go?"

"Yeah, please, can we go?" Hawke asked with the same puppy eyes his son had.

"You two drive a hard bargain." She nodded, although there was no question about whether or not she'd go. If she was going to keep Hawke in her life, she needed to meet his friends and do whatever it took to ensure he'd have the best relationship with his son, regardless of what happened with her and Hawke, though things did look pretty promising.

"Mind if I have a word with Hawke alone?" Arthur asked.

"Not at all." Calista rested her hand on her son's back. "We'll be inside. Say thank you to Arthur."

"Thanks!" David raised his fist, and Arthur pounded it. "I'm going to go text Justice and tell him I'm going!"

"I'm sure he'll be happy about that, David," Arthur said.

"I like being called David." David glanced between her and Hawke.

"It's a good name," Calista said.

David smiled and raced into the house.

"I'll leave you two alone." As gracefully as she could, she entered the kitchen where her son stood with his hands on his hips.

"Are you and Daddy together?"

These were questions she'd rather not field just yet, but since she got caught with her hand in the cookie jar, she needed to devise something that would satisfy her son's natural curiosity and wouldn't make her and Hawke the couple of the month.

"Have you had breakfast? I can make some pancakes or French toast."

"I've already eaten." There was a tremble in David's voice as if he were holding back tears. "Are you and Daddy going to be a couple?"

"Your father and I haven't seen each other in ten years. When he left Dover, we weren't on the best of terms, but seeing each other again, well, it's hard not to have feelings, but that doesn't make us a couple."

"Then why were you sitting on his lap and kissing him?"

Hawke wanted to date. Well, now he would get his chance because she would never break her kid's heart.

Or hers.

Not if she could help it.

"Your dad and I are going to try our hand at

dating and see where it takes us." For the first time in ten years, Calista felt as though she wouldn't go through this journey alone.

8

"What am I looking at?" Hawke took the folder that Arthur handed him but didn't open it. He leaned against the railing across from where Arthur stood. The hot Florida sun beat down on his back, which itched from the new words added to his tattoo.

But his family truly had control of his heart.

Arthur had a somber look etched on his face. His jaw was relaxed, but his lips were pulled tight, and a crinkle wiggled across his forehead, showing off his age. "An official complaint about you."

"Me? What the hell did I do? And to whom did I do it?" A few years back, Hawke got into it with a fellow firefighter who was an asshole. One night, after a few drinks, Hawke had enough of Jonathon's chauvinist ways, and Hawke punched him, more than once.

The next morning, Jonathon filed a formal complaint, and Hawke ended up suspended for a week, and the altercation would forever be in his record, especially since Hawke had done some real damage to Jonathon's face.

However, he'd kept his nose clean since then.

"Wendel Lawrence. He said that you assaulted him at his son's school," Arthur said.

"You've got to be kidding me." Hawke flipped open the file and scanned the report.

"He's got a witness."

"I see that." Hawke flipped the page. He rolled the name *Riley Simpson* around in his brain, but nothing came up. "I punched the man once, that's it. I wouldn't call it assault. And the asshole just laughed anyway. Duncan was there. He'll file a statement on my behalf."

"I already had him file one this morning, but it doesn't matter. You hit him."

"Who is this Riley Simpson person?" Hawke asked.

"She's a single mother. A widow, from what I've learned, has her sights set on Wendel as her next husband. They have been out a few times, but Wendel goes out with many women."

"Why would anyone want to be with that asshole?"

"I haven't a single clue." Arthur rested his hand on Hawke's shoulder like an older brother giving advice would. "Kaelie's closing in on him, but he's filed a formal complaint against her too."

"She did get in his face a couple of months ago."

"And last night," Arthur said.

"What the hell did she do now?"

Normally, Kaelie never lost her cool, and she had the best resting bitch face known to man. But she was a shark, and he'd hate to be on the wrong side of her questions during an interrogation.

"She ran into him while he was out on a date with Riley."

"Ran into? Or planned? Because she didn't leave here until nearly eight last night."

Arthur arched his brow. "Let's go with ran into. Anyway, she went up to them and said hello. Then she leaned in and whispered in his ear that she was days from arresting him. According to the waitress, Kaelie accidentally spilled wine all over his lap."

"Nothing Kaelie does is an accident," Hawke said.

"It gets better."

Hawke could only imagine.

"While she frantically tried to clean up the mess, a file dropped from her purse right in Riley's lap. Inside was a picture of the last victim wearing a necklace that is found on every victim, a little-known fact that hasn't been released to the public."

"She's taunting him," Hawke said.

"She wants to catch him before someone else dies, so she's trying to make him squirm."

"I'd say she's doing a damn good job." Hawke knew very little about how investigations were handled. Other than being friends with Kaelie and her husband, Hawke's role as a paramedic and fire-fighter didn't require that skill set.

Nor did he want the responsibility.

But now that his family was involved, even peripherally, he wanted every detail and to be immersed in the case.

"Kaelie is good at her job, but she's letting this one get to her. Hits too close to home with her sister's murder," Arthur said.

"Every murder she hears about hits her that way, but this one is worse because she's investigating a fire where evidence was found, making her part of the equation." It was something he could understand since every death by suicide or attempted suicide brought him right back to the day they found Courtney's body and the letter she left behind. "Did Wendel file complaints about anyone else?"

Arthur laughed. "Me and Rex over how we handled the investigation of the fire at his house, but since its ongoing, nothing will happen with it other than a little pressure from the chief to wrap it up. And yours, all that will happen at this point is you'll need to sit with a case worker and explain your side, but—"

"He's got his cop buddies listening to his side, and he wants assault charges. He doesn't want this to be an internal department thing." Hawke didn't need to be an investigator to figure that out.

"Flip to the last page of that report." Arthur folded his arms across his chest.

There, in the back of the file, was a picture of Wendel with a black eye, a bruised cheek, and a cut lip. "I didn't do that," Hawke said. "I hit him in the belly, and not even full force."

"He's got a witness that says otherwise, and he looked like that when Kaelie saw him, so don't be surprised if the local police come knocking at your door."

"Why would they waste their time on a case like this? It's just two blokes exchanging a few fists. Who the fuck cares?"

"It happened on school property for one and two"—Arthur took the folder, fingered through the pages until he pulled one out, and held it up—"he has this threatening email from you."

"What? He's the one who sent me a hostile note." Hawke took the paper between his fingers and read the report.

"Watch your back, buddy. If you think what happened today was bad, you wait. It's all being set up. You will rot in prison. You know what they do to men who rape women, right? It's just a matter of time. I've got it all worked out."

"That's my email address, in response to his email, which has been altered, but I didn't send that." Hawke scrunched the paper in his fist. "He's seriously trying to make it look like I'm setting him up?"

"You're missing the bigger picture. He's setting you up as the rapist and murderer."

Hawke opened his mouth, but nothing came out.

"That's fucking crazy, and he won't be able to do it."

"Kaelie wants you to give her and Rusty full access to your email voluntarily so they can disprove this immediately."

"Done." Hawke's phone vibrated in his back pocket. He took a moment to clear his throat and pulled out his cell.

Hawke glanced at the screen. "It's my landlord." He tapped the green answer button and set it on speaker. "Hello?"

"Sorry to bother you, but I was just handed a search warrant for your house." His heart raced as all the blood in his body boiled. "I'll be right there." He stared at Arthur who pinched the bridge of his nose.

"You didn't go home last night," Arthur said as a statement. "Rusty had someone drive by here last night and my place a few times, but not yours."

"Is anyone following Wendel? It should be easy to dispute all of this."

"Rusty's really struggling with this. Wendel has friends. And no one likes it when one of their own is accused. Rusty has a handful of men and women he can trust. So, no cops have been following Wendel. I called Timothy, and we've got eyes on him through the Aegis Network, but there are gaps."

"Shit," Hawke mumbled. "I've got to get to my place."

"I'll drive, and on the way, I'll make sure Rusty, Kaelie, and Timothy all know what's going on."

"Give me a minute." Hawke made his way to the kitchen, contemplating what he would say. He'd been looking forward to spending as much time with Calista and David as possible, even if that meant spending it with most of his entire team. He wanted Calista to see he had a good life here and that it would be worth giving it a go.

God, he hoped she wanted to spend the rest of their lives making up for his stupid mistake.

But he'd have to win her over, and running out on her and David wasn't the way to do that.

"What's wrong?" Calista asked.

"Yeah. You look like you saw a ghost or something," David said.

As perceptive as his mother. "My landlord called. Something happened at my place. I've got to head over there." He found a piece of paper and a pen. "Here's the address of my buddy Rex's house and yacht. His wife's name is Tilly. She's a real gem, and you'll love her."

Calista nodded.

He set his keys on the counter. "You can take my pickup if you want."

"You're leaving it here?" Calista asked.

"If you don't mind. Arthur and I are going to my house together."

"Sure thing," she said. "Is everything okay?"

"Yeah. It's nothing. Just a leaky pipe."

Calista cocked her head back.

He might be able to tell her the truth, but he didn't want to worry David.

"Trust me," he whispered, pulling Calista in for a quick kiss, and then he hugged his son. He held him for a long moment, closing his eyes and resting his nose against the top of his head. He smelled like innocence on top of a decadent chocolate cake.

No way would he let anyone destroy what he'd just found. "You take good care of your mom, you hear?"

"Yes, sir," David said, glancing up with a big smile. "Thanks for finding us."

"Thank you for forgiving me for not being around. I can't really make up for all the lost time, but I'm going to do my best."

"I love you, Dad."

Salty tears stung the corners of his eyes. Never

in a million years did he think he'd hear those words.

Nor did he believe he could ever love someone as much as he loved this boy. "I love you right back." In a matter of a day, David had become Hawke's world.

"Do you know what they are looking for?" Hawke asked Rusty as he stood in his front yard, not caring that half the neighborhood had come out and were all conversing on the street, pointing and staring.

"The warrant isn't specific other than we have the right to seize anything they deem pertinent to the case," Rusty said as he snapped on a pair of latex gloves.

"How does me hitting Wendel once constitute a case and a search warrant?"

"It doesn't," Rusty said. "Do you know a woman by the name Denise Cannon?"

Hawke nodded. "I took her out a few times a couple of months ago."

"She was raped last night."

"Jesus Christ," he mumbled. His heart sank to the pit of his stomach, stirring up acid and sending it to the back of his throat. He gagged. "Was she murdered?"

"She's in the hospital. Her neighbor had stopped by and saw her on the floor with a plastic bag over her head."

"Is that how the victims were killed?" Hawke rubbed the back of his neck as he watched a local detective carry out his laptop, followed by a uniformed officer carrying a box.

Rusty nodded. "What sucks for you is that we never released how the bodies were found, so no one knows about the plastic bag but those I told, first responders, and the killer."

"Was her attacker still in the house?"

"He ran out the back door. We've got a print of his shoes in the mud, and he also left behind some duct tape," Rusty said. "What shoe size are you?"

"Are you seriously going to ask me that?" His heart pounded so fast he couldn't tell when one heartbeat ended and another one started.

Rusty cocked his head.

"Thirteen," he said under his breath.

"Well, that's good because the print we have is a size eleven, but the bad news is that the neighbor, when asked for a description, said it was closer to you than to Wendel."

"Does the neighbor know Wendel?" Hawke's mind raced with a million questions. He tried to sort through all of them, prioritizing them, but they spun around like alphabet soup in a blender. "Who is the neighbor?" Hawke remembered when he'd dropped Denise off after a disastrous date, but only because he realized she wanted a husband and not a fling, a woman had been walking her dog and stopped to talk to Denise and him, but he couldn't remember her name.

"Riley Simpson," Rusty said with a smirk.

"The eyewitness who says I beat the crap out of Wendel? The same one who was on a date with him last night?"

"Wendel is getting desperate, and he's making mistakes," Rusty said. "I'm sorry about Denise, but we're confident she'll pull through."

"She's a nice girl and doesn't deserve this."

"No one does."

"What if they find something Wendel might have planted in my house?" Hawke pointed to the detective and officer standing in his driveway, glaring over their shoulders.

"I think they already have," Rusty said. "There's a little misplaced loyalty when it comes to one two of these officers here. Deep down, they good cops and I know they have their doubts about what kind of police officer Wendel is. They've seen him in action and know he's dangerous. But no one likes to admit one of their own is actually one of those really bad people you want behind bars. Even I don't like that."

"That's not making me feel any better."

"In about five minutes, they will get a phone call telling them to turn everything over to me. That I am now the lead detective on these cases."

"How did you manage that? I thought you were just sticking your nose in where it didn't belong."

"Detective Brown asked for my help months ago, so I've always been on the case. But Wendel has been pushing Brown's buttons, and recently, he went to our captain over something stupid. Brown had enough and told the cap that he thought I was better equipped and had been working on the case all along. Pissed Wendel right the fuck off because he knows he can't control me."

"He tried to manipulate Brown?"

"That's what Brown said." Rusty nodded. "But still working on everything. I need him. dealing with this from day one. But he'll kground."

ved his hands deep in his pockets,

swallowing the vile taste this entire thing has left in his mouth. "Here they come."

"This is going to get weird, real fast," Rusty said, waving to Arthur.

Arthur nodded and jogged in their direction.

"Answer their questions. Don't lie about anything," Rusty said. "Don't be a hothead."

"Are you Hawke Wilson?" the police officer asked.

"I am." He held out his hand and gave the man a firm handshake. He puffed out his chest. Not so much as a form of a pissing contest, but mostly to keep himself tall and proud. It also helped that Arthur stood at his side.

"And you live here?"

"I do."

"Do you know why we're here?" the police officer asked.

"You seem to think I might have something to do with the rape of an old girlfriend of mine." It was a stretch to call her that, but they had dated for a month, and he had slept with her a few times, so it seemed to be fitting.

"That and the assault on Wendel Lawrence," the police officer said.

"That's not why we're here," Rusty said.

"Officer Hardy, you're going to null and void this search if you bring in the accusations of the assault to Wendel. It's not part of our warrant, and the two cases are unrelated. Since we're standing here chatting, I need a log of what was taken from Hawke's home."

Hawke had to admit, it was kind of fun to watch Rusty in action, though he would prefer it not be about him.

"If you'd like to come over and check out the evidence, feel free, but…" Hardy pulled out his cell and frowned. "Will you excuse me a minute?"

"Sure thing," Rusty said. "I wish I didn't take any pleasure in this. I remember being a cop and enjoying playing detective before I became one. They have no idea why Brown isn't here and I am. They won't like this."

"I seriously don't understand the politics of this," Hawke said.

"It's simple. A few months back, Wendel did something in the line of duty that nearly got me killed. I'm vocal about how I feel about that man being a cop. Me taking on the rape cases will cause waves. But the captain's seen Kaelie's report. The evidence is compelling. He wants someone who will be willing to cuff one of their own or walk away if it's not him. That man is me."

"This is a fucking nightmare." Hawke ran his fingers through his hair.

"This is all going to blow over," Arthur said, slapping him on the back. "Besides, this isn't the right neighborhood to raise a young man in. I think you'd do best to move into Calista's place."

"You've got me married already?" The word *married* rolled off his tongue a little too easily. He swallowed.

He actually liked the idea.

It warmed his heart.

For the first time in ten years, he felt alive.

And terrified at the same time.

Hardy shook his head. "How did you manage to take this case from Brown?"

"I didn't take anything. It was assigned. Now, instead of standing here pounding our chests, let's get to work."

"That's what I've been doing. Everything we collected is in the back of the van. Benny's got the log." Hardy relaxed his stance. "Can I ask you a question?"

"Sure." Rusty nodded.

"I need to know if Brown walked off this case or if something happened."

Rusty cocked his head.

Hardy let out a long breath. "Look, man. We've got a rapist and murderer on our hands and one of our own has been suspended. I know what it's looked like here all morning. Trust me, I don't like searching a first responder's home any more than I like wondering if a man that wears the same badge as I do is a criminal."

Hawke glanced toward Arthur.

"No offense, Hardy. But you don't act like you wonder any such thing," Rusty said.

"I'm a beat cop. I do what I'm told. But I went to the captain a couple of months ago about a concern I had over Wendel. He's a fucking loose cannon. I keep my distance from him, and if you thought my attitude here was about that, you're dead wrong. I was just doing my job. Collecting evidence, whether it makes sense or not. But Brown is a good detective and Wendel tried to get to him."

Rusty let out a slow breath. "How do I know you're not full of shit?"

"My kid goes to school with Wendel's kid."

"Then mine as well," Hawke said.

Hardy nodded. "The only reason I brought up

the assault charges was because I was there that day and know it's bogus."

"Why didn't you say that sooner?" Rusty planted his hands on his hips. "That's the whole reason I don't trust you right now."

"You didn't give me a chance," Hardy said. "I don't trust Wendel and I sure as shit don't think he's a good guy. So, do you want to go over what we pulled from Hawke's house?"

"I do." Rusty nodded.

"Because of an email we found at the victim's home from Hawke—"

"I haven't sent an email to Denise in months. Hell, I haven't seen her in months," Hawke said, interrupting Hardy.

"Let him finish," Rusty demanded in an authoritative tone.

"Because of that, we had an order to seize his computer or any other tablet we could find. We also found the same type of plastic bags that were used to cover Denise's face along with the same brand of tape that was used to bound her wrists and ankles."

"Tape? What tape?" Hawke asked. "Because yesterday I went to get some duct tape, and I'm all out."

"There was a half-used roll on your kitchen

countertop," Hardy said. "It matches what we found at the scene."

Hawke's heart dropped to his stomach. "The only thing I left there was a bunch of letters and pictures of my son."

Hardy shook his head. "There were no letters or images in the kitchen. Are you sure?"

"It's a long story, but yesterday morning, after I opened the letters, I left them to talk to my son and his mother. I didn't know they were in town. Hell, I didn't know I had a kid until yesterday, and I left all the pictures Calista sent me on the counter. I haven't been home since."

Out of the corner of Hawke's eye, he saw Zach and Noah race from their backyard.

Hawke knew he could use all the support he could get.

"If that asshole stole the pictures of my son or my letters, I'm going to fucking—"

Arthur held up his hand. "I would stop that sentence now, if you know what is good for you."

"Was there any sign of forced entry anywhere?" Hawke asked, knowing damn well he locked the door. Zach always harassed him about being anal-retentive about locked doors.

Zach had a point, but it had been a habit

Hawke's father had ingrained into his head since he was a small child and their house had been burglarized.

"None that we could find," the detective said. "But one of my officers said the back door was unlocked."

Hawke forced his mind to go back to two days ago. He recounted the steps of the hour before he left for his twenty-four-hour shift. He was a creature of habit and liked his routines. That morning, he'd gotten up, made himself some coffee, and sat on the back patio and read the news before going back inside and locking the door.

He remembered that detail specifically and when he'd returned home yesterday morning, he hadn't even gone out the back door.

The only people who had a key to his place were Noah and Zach.

"Hey, Zach," Hawke called, waving him over. "Bring Noah too."

"What's going on?" Rusty asked.

"I'm positive I locked that door, but they have a key, not that they would go in my house without asking, but I gave them one for emergencies. They also can see my house from their backyard, especially when the landlord trims back the bushes, which he did a few weeks ago." Hawke turned his attention to Zach and Noah. "Did either of you go into my house or see anyone?"

"We left yesterday afternoon to go fishing and slept on the boat. Just got home about a half hour ago," Zach said.

"One of the neighbors said they saw the cable company parked in your driveway yesterday around three," Detective Hardy said.

"At three I was at my girlfriend's house with our son. We had just picked up David after he had an altercation with Wendel's son." Hawke felt sorry for that poor, misguided boy, and he worried about what might happen to him when his father was busted for rape and murder.

That would a horrible legacy to deal with, and in that moment, Hawke decided that when this was over, he was going to do his best to make sure that kid understood no one blamed him for his father's actions.

He could only hope that Calista and David would be on board after everything that had happened.

"I can account for my every move in the last twenty-four hours. I've either been with my buddy Duncan or my girlfriend and son," Hawke said.

"And I didn't call the cable company, so why were they parked in my driveway?"

"We've got a call in to them to find out," Hardy said. "Shall I forward that call to you, Rusty?"

"Just give me the report," he said, holding up a piece of paper. "This warrant is only for Hawke's computer. You had no right to go looking anywhere else for evidence."

"The tape was on the counter, and I had probable cause, and you know it," Hardy said. "What are the chances Hawke's prints are on them?"

"Slim to none," Hawke said with an exasperated sigh. "While you're at it, dust for prints on my back door."

"We'll be sure to do that," Rusty said in a reassuring tone.

"For the record, this smells like a bad setup," Hardy said. "Timelines don't add up. I've been doing this a long time; this is too easy. Too many tiny details that usually take time to uncover were laid out for us, right down to a scratch on your truck."

"That's a specific detail, but I fixed that the other day."

"I've got it," Rusty said, holding up his cell.

"Got what?" Hawke asked.

"We've got a DNA match linking Wendel to two of the victims."

"That's great. That means all of this means absolutely nothing," Hawke said, letting out a sigh of relief.

"I wish. We still have to work through this investigation because it's not necessarily related right now," Rusty said. "Let's walk through your house."

"Rusty, put us to work." Zach slapped Hawke on the back. "Because we take care of our own."

9

Calista stood in front of her closet. What the hell did one bring on a yacht? She made the mistake of Googling the address and holy crap. The marina where Hawke's friend kept his yacht was right out of the rich and famous. When he'd said the word *yacht* before and when Arthur mentioned all the toys, it hadn't really sunk in that she'd be going on a real yacht.

More like a mini cruise ship.

She'd changed her bathing suit and cover-up three times and still wasn't satisfied. "Mom, we're going to be late," David called from the family room.

"That's my line." She grabbed her beach bag and tossed it over her shoulder. "How do I look?"

"You're the prettiest mom in the world."

"Thanks. Shall we take Hawke's truck?"

"Can you drive something that big?" David asked with wide eyes.

"Want to hear something funny?" Tossing her arm around her son and leading him to the front door, she let herself remember everything good about Hawke and all the reasons why she'd fallen in love with him.

And why she still loved him.

Most would call him an alpha male. Strong and quiet but commanding at the same time. And he was all that. But she knew the real Hawke. The Hawke she knew was loving and sweet and had a soft spot in his heart for the world. He didn't show it to most, but she'd seen how sensitive he could be.

"Hawke's first truck, I had to teach him how to parallel park it."

"No way!"

"He was so proud of that truck." He'd been heartbroken when Courtney had mutilated it, but the body shop had done an excellent job of making it look like new again. "He'd been saving for the down payment since high school."

"What did he drive before that?"

"An old beat-up hatchback. It was the ugliest

thing I'd ever seen. I was happy for him when he bought himself something a little nicer. I begged him to let me drive, but he wouldn't hear of it, until he tried to park. I bet him a hundred dollars that I could do it on the first try."

"Did you do it?"

She nodded. "He still owes me a hundred bucks." She laughed as she curled her fingers around the doorknob and yanked it open.

Her laugh caught in her throat. "Hawke. You're back?"

"And for the record, I can parallel park Marthy," he said with a stupid grin.

"Marthy?" David asked.

"Your father has always named his cars. The truck he had when we were dating was LuAnndra. That was his second truck." She shook her head at the memory. "Dumbest name for a vehicle ever."

"How do you decide on the names?" David looped his arm around Hawke's waist, glancing up at him with doe-like eyes.

Calista tapped her index finger against her chest in unison with her beating heart. Joy spread across her body like the warmth of the sun heating her face. She'd dreamed about this day for years, only the reality was better than anything she'd imagined.

Her phone dinged.

She dug it out of her oversized purse and frowned. "It's my emergency line." For the most part, Calista had always been able to leave work at the office, and other than the nights she covered the suicide hotline, she rarely dealt with her patients outside of their hour on her couch.

And being new in town, she didn't have too many clients. But she had a few and she couldn't ignore them.

She tapped the accept button. "This is Calista Alba."

"We have a Rick Rosen on the line. He's indicated that he's got a bottle of pills and is about to take them."

"I need a minute before you connect me." Calista covered the phone. "I have to take this, and I could be a while. It's an emergency and it's private."

"Why don't I take David, and you call me when you're done? Even if Rex takes the yacht off the docks, I can come to get you on one of the Jet Skis or the little boat." Hawke took the beach bag and handed it to their son. "David, take this and toss it in the back seat, then climb in. I'll be there in a sec."

"Okay, Dad. I love you, Mom."

"I'll be there soon, promise," she said, waving. "Are you sure you don't mind?" she asked, pressing the phone to her ear.

"He's my son. I'll never mind spending time with him. Or his mother, but I've seen that look before." Hawke traced his finger along the side of her face. "Your eyes used to go from a shiny blue to a dull shade, and you would crinkle your nose like you're doing right now every time Courtney would threaten to kill herself."

A sharp pain poked through her chest right to the center of her heart. "I got so tired of her threats. I ignored all the classic signs the last time."

"How many of your patients are suicidal?" Hawke asked.

"That's my specialty."

"So I tortured myself one way, and you do it another way."

She curled her fingers around his thick biceps. "No, Hawke. I don't work with this type of client because I want to punish myself. I do it because as Courtney's best friend, I couldn't help her. She needed a professional. I'm that professional for everyone who has a friend that needs help. And I suspect you continued with your medical training and became a paramedic and firefighter in your civilian life because you wanted to help people who are incapable, for whatever reason, of doing it themselves."

"I never looked at it that way before." He pressed his lips against her temple. "I'm sorry for everything."

"I know you are," she whispered. "We can't go back, but we can be a family going forward."

"Does that include dating?"

She let out a short laugh. "Call me crazy, but yes."

He cupped her cheeks. "No matter what the future holds, I won't ever walk away from you and our son again. That's a promise you can count on."

"Go. I'll see you soon."

"Rusty has cars driving through the neighborhood and the Aegis Network has someone lurking around Wendel. You'll be safe."

"Thanks." For the next thirty seconds, she stood in the driveway and waved to the man she had never stopped loving and their son. This moment was worth every tear she had shed for the last ten years. "Patch Rick through," she said to her after-hours service provider.

Calista stepped inside and headed toward the kitchen for another cup of coffee.

"I can't do this anymore," Rick said with a raspy voice.

"Where are…" Calista stopped mid-step between her family room and kitchen. "What the hell?" she whispered, staring at Wendel. He leaned against her counter with a smug grin.

"Hello, Calista."

The inflection of his voice rose an octave, causing the hair on the back of her neck to stand straight up.

Something shiny resting on the counter caught her attention.

A gun.

She dropped her hand to her side, and her cell phone crashed onto the floor. "What are you doing here?"

"Your new boyfriend and his buddies are making my life miserable, and thanks to him, one of my own detectives and some damn fire investigator are at my house right now with a search warrant. Vile little bitch, that one."

"Kaelie?" Calista swallowed the fear that had slithered its way up from the pit of her stomach. She needed to snap her mind into action. She had no idea what this man wanted, but she didn't think his motives were pure, especially since he took the gun in his hand and pointed it at her chest.

Think.

Breathe.

Stay calm.

Communicate.

"My ex-wife showed up a half hour ago with papers giving her temporary full custody until this matter is taken care of, and it's all your fault."

"I'm sorry your ex did that. I'm sure it was very troubling." She clasped her hands together, squeezing tight to keep them from shaking.

"Do you know what it's like to have your kid taken away from you?"

Her chest tightened, and for a second, she thought her heart had stopped beating. "What have you done with my son?" she asked behind a clenched jaw.

"I haven't done anything to him, yet. But he will be scarred for life."

She lunged forward but skidded to a stop when he held his weapon in her face.

"While I'm fucking you right here in your own kitchen, Hawke will be off having a good time, but I'm going to come forward with information that I believed he was going to try to hurt his son because of our relationship."

She'd dealt with many narcissistic sociopaths before, but not one this dangerous. Staring past the twinkle in his eye and his bright smile, she knew without a doubt this man was capable of murder. He was the kind of man who believed all of his actions were justified, no matter the cost to someone else.

That meant he wouldn't hesitate to pull the trigger if it helped his end game.

It also meant there was no reasoning with him. No talking him down. No trying to get him to see the errors of his ways.

Basically, she was fucked.

"You really think that's what people are going to believe?" she asked.

"Of course they are because I'll have pictures of us, showing the world how passionate you are when you're with me."

She laughed, which she shouldn't have since he pressed the gun to her temple, causing her to gag, vomiting a little in her throat. "You touch me, and I'll fight back, and not a single picture you manage to take will look like I'm having any kind of pleasure at all."

"I've taken more than one woman before, and let me tell you a little something about the female body." He leaned in closer, his nose so close to her skin that she felt the heat of his breath right down to her toes. "It betrays you every time. I bet your nipples are tightening and sending a warm throbbing right here." He cupped her between the legs, rubbing his finger against her.

A rumble at the pit of her stomach twisted and turned. The disgust at his touch turned her body cold. She grabbed his wrist and yanked as hard as she could, taking a step back. "You're going to have to kill me because I will never let you have me. I will kick, scream, bite, dig my nails into your skin, leaving marks—"

"Of passion, because we know you like it rough."

"You're seriously delusional." Taunting a raging lunatic wasn't something anyone would recommend. However, if she pegged Wendel's psychology correctly, rape before murder was a necessity. "Tell me something, Wendel. How many women have you raped and killed?"

"What makes you think I've ever killed anyone?" The way he smiled reminded her of Ted Bundy.

She shivered. "You raped and killed all those women the news has been talking about, haven't you?"

"Even if I did, which I'm not admitting to, why would I tell you?" He inched closer until her back was up against the wall.

"Because if you even try to rape me, you'll have to kill me."

"But that's the beauty of it. I won't be the one killing you. It will be Hawke."

She gasped. "That's impossible."

"Is it? Because he left here with your son, without you, heading to his rich friend's yacht after he raped and killed you."

"You haven't thought this through. Your DNA will be all over me. The pictures will be time-stamped. Everyone will see that you did this, not Hawke."

"I'm a powerful man; it will be easy to doctor the evidence. The only regret I'm going to have is that you won't be alive to see it destroy your son and to watch Hawke get shackled and taken to prison."

He rammed his knee between her legs.

She pounded his chest with her fists and managed to push from the wall, but no sooner did she maneuver around him than he yanked her back by her hair.

"Let me go." She cocked her arm and elbowed him in the gut.

"Not smart," he said, slamming her face forward into the wall. He stood behind her, pressing his disgusting body against hers.

Taking in a deep breath, she contemplated her next move. No matter what she did, she ran the risk of the gun going off.

Wendel licked the side of her face with his slimy tongue. "You repulse me." She pushed back as hard as she could, giving her just enough space to twist her body and kick his shin.

"Fucking cunt." He hobbled backward. "You're going to pay for that."

Panic squeezed her heart as she headed for the family room. She needed to get out of the house. Her neighbors were always outside, so all she had to do was go running and screaming, and someone would help her.

A strong arm came around her stomach.

She turned and swung, landing her fist right in the center of Wendel's nose.

A second later, something cold smashed against the side of her face. Her vision blurred as she dropped to her knees. A sharp pain radiated across her head and down the back of her neck. She blinked, trying to focus, but her peripheral vision became smaller and smaller. She fought the darkness threatening to take over.

She had to fight.

She would fight.

To the bitter end.

Hopefully it wouldn't be her end.

The taste of metal dribbled down her throat.

"See what you made me do?" Wendel lifted her to a standing position by her shoulders.

Her legs wobbled as if she were a newborn horse trying to gain his balance for the very first time. She saw two of everything but focused her gaze on the gun. She'd have the upper hand if she could get the gun from him.

"Bend over the sofa," he commanded as he shoved her, turning her body. He pressed his hand on the small of her back, pushing the top part of her body.

She gripped the back of the couch. One of his hands slipped down between her legs while the other one rested next to her hand, with the gun.

Get the weapon. That's all she had to do.

She took in a long breath, letting it out slowly.

"That's it, baby, relax. You're going to love this."

"You might be right," she whispered.

For a second, he froze.

She took that opportunity to reach for his weapon with both hands. The metal felt cold to the touch. Yanking it from his hands, she butted him with her ass, sending him backward. He lost his footing and fell to the floor. "I'd stay there if I were you." With a shaky hand, she aimed the gun at his heart.

"You won't shoot me," Wendel said just as the front door flew open.

"She won't, but these cops will." Kaelie stepped to the side as two armed officers raced past her.

"You're under arrest," Rusty said as he hoisted Wendel to his feet, pulling his hands behind his back and cuffing them.

"Are you okay?" Kaelie asked, gently taking the gun from Calista's hand.

Calista nodded. "How did you know to come here?"

"Your call never ended with your patient. He called 9-1-1." Kaelie guided her toward the kitchen, eased her onto one of the chairs, and pointed to the phone.

The last thing Calista wanted to do was cry, but she couldn't stop the tears from rolling down her cheeks. "Where's my son?"

"He's with Arthur, heading toward the yacht. Hawke's on his way back here."

Calista watched as the officers continued to read Wendel his rights.

"You better get that piece of shit out of here before Hawke gets back," Calista said. "He has a wicked temper."

No sooner did she say that than Hawke appeared in the front door, his hands already forming fists.

"You fucking asshole," Hawke yelled, lunging forward.

Rusty stepped in his way, but Hawke just shoved him aside like a sack of potatoes.

"I'm telling you, Calista is quite the piece of ass," Wendel said with that same stupid grin he always sported.

Hawke cocked his arm.

"Let him do it," Rusty said. "One swing. Just turn your backs."

The other officer stepped aside and turned away.

Hawke's fist landed on Wendel's nose, making a crackling sound.

"You can't let him do that!" Wendel stumbled backward, holding his bloody nose.

"Do what? I didn't see anything, did you?" Rusty asked. "Calista must have done that while you were trying to rape her."

"That's what I thought," the other officer said as he took Wendel by the arm and hauled him out of the house.

"That wasn't necessary," Calista said softly.

Hawke knelt, running his finger across her forehead.

She winced.

"Okay, maybe he deserved it," she said.

"Damn right he did," Kaelie said. "I'll be outside. The ambulance should be here any minute."

"I'm so sorry I left you." Hawke held her gaze. "I should have waited."

"No. If you hadn't, David would have been here, and I wouldn't have wanted him to see what just happened. It's going to be horrifying enough when he sees my face. Is it bad?"

"Let's just say you'll need at least five stitches, but you're still the prettiest woman in any room."

"Flattery will get you everywhere." Her head throbbed, and she still couldn't see straight. A wave of dizziness made the world go black for a second. "I'm a little woozy," she said.

"I'm pretty sure you have a concussion."

"That sucks."

Hawke let out a slight chuckle. "Here come the paramedics. Let's get you on the gurney and to the hospital."

"Is that really necessary?"

"It is. I'll call David and let him know you're okay. Do you want me to have someone bring him to the hospital or have him stay with Arthur?"

"Let him have fun. Why don't you go too? I'm fine."

"I'm never leaving you again. Ever. You're stuck with me for the rest of your life. I want more than to co-parent our kid. I want us." He brushed a piece of her hair from her face. "I love you, Calista. I always have, and I always will. I mean it. Now tell me you love me and that you'll marry me."

"If I say it now, it's just the concussion talking."

Hawke helped her up onto the gurney. She lay back, closing her eyes. All she wanted to do was sleep and dream about a world where Hawke wanted her to be his wife.

Someone tapped at her shoulder. "Say yes."

"I love you, Hawke. Always have. Always will," she whispered. She fought to keep her eyes open, but the bright sun made her head explode. She heard voices as the paramedics lifted her into the back of the ambulance, but she couldn't make out the words.

All she knew was that Hawke was at her side, holding her hand…

And he loved her.

"Yes," she whispered.

EPILOGUE

ONE MONTH LATER...

"Good morning, husband."

If someone had told Hawke just a few months ago that he would be a married man with a ten-year-old kid, he would have laughed so hard it would have given him a hernia. He set his mug on the counter and poured himself a cup of coffee, smiling. "Hello, wife." The warm tropical ocean breeze filtered through the open sliding glass windows of their private bungalow in Key West. "We've been married now for eighteen hours."

"What do you want to do on our one-day anniversary?" Calista looped her arms around his waist and nuzzled her face in his neck, her plump lips pressing hot against his skin.

"Go back to bed."

She laughed. "This morning in the shower wasn't enough for you?"

"You'll always be more than enough." He ran his fingers through her long hair and took a deep breath, inhaling the sweet smell of coconuts. He cupped her face, tilting her head back. Her loving gaze captivated him, sucking out all the oxygen from his lungs. "You know, we should think about having another kid." He hadn't meant to blurt that out, but it had been in the back of his mind ever since he proposed. Of course, she made him do it again when she wasn't lying in an ambulance while semiconscious.

"Is that what you want?"

"We're pushing forty. While it's not insanely old, it's not young either. I get that there would be a huge age difference with a new baby and David, but so what. Do you think he'll be okay with the idea?"

"What do you think, Dad?"

Hawke smiled. "Yeah. He'd be agreeable. Now what about you?"

"Well, *Dad*, I think I can make a baby happen in about seven months."

"I thought it took nine?"

Calista arched a playful brow.

"You can't be serious. You're pregnant?"

"Happy one-day anniversary, husband."

Thank you so much for taking the time to read HAWKE'S HONOR. Please feel free to leave an honest review.

If you haven't had the chance to read any the Orlando Branch of the Aegis Network, check them out!

THE AEGIS NETWORK

The Sarich Brother

The Lighthouse

Her Last Hope

The Last Flight

The Return Home

The Matriarch

Grab a glass of vino, kick back, relax, and let the romance roll in…

Sign up for my Newsletter (https://dl.bookfunnel.com/ 82gm8b9k4y) where I often give away free books before publication.

Join my private Facebook group (https://www.facebook. com/groups/191706547909047/) where I post exclusive excerpts and discuss all things murder and love!

ABOUT THE AUTHOR

Jen Talty is the *USA Today* Bestselling Author of Contemporary Romance, Romantic Suspense, and Paranormal Romance. In the fall of 2020, her short story was selected and featured in a 1001 Dark Nights Anthology.

Regardless of the genre, her goal is to take you on a ride that will leave you floating under the sun with warmth in your heart. She writes stories about broken heroes and heroines who aren't necessarily looking for romance, but in the end, they find the kind of love books are written about :).

She first started writing while carting her kids to one hockey rink after the other, averaging 170 games per year between 3 kids in 2 countries and 5 states. Her first book, IN TWO WEEKS was originally published in 2007. In 2010 she helped form a publishing company (Cool Gus Publishing) with *NY*

Times Bestselling Author Bob Mayer where she ran the technical side of the business through 2016.

Jen is currently enjoying the next phase of her life…the empty nester! She and her husband reside in Jupiter, Florida.

Grab a glass of vino, kick back, relax, and let the romance roll in…

    Sign up for my Newsletter (https://dl.bookfunnel.com/82gm8b9k4y), where I often give away free books before publication.

    Join my private Facebook group (https://www.facebook.com/groups/191706547909047/) where I post exclusive excerpts and discuss all things murder and love!

Never miss a new release. Follow me on Amazon:amazon.com/author/jentalty

    And on Bookbub: bookbub.com/authors/jentalty

ALSO BY JEN TALTY

Brand new series: SAFE HARBOR!

Mine To Keep

Mine To Save

Mine To Protect

Mine to Hold

Mine to Love

Check out LOVE IN THE ADIRONDACKS!

Shattered Dreams

An Inconvenient Flame

The Wedding Driver

Clear Blue Sky

Blue Moon

Before the Storm

NY STATE TROOPER SERIES (also set in the Adirondacks!)

In Two Weeks

Dark Water

Deadly Secrets

Murder in Paradise Bay

To Protect His own

Deadly Seduction

When A Stranger Calls

His Deadly Past

The Corkscrew Killer

First Responders: A spin-off from the NY State Troopers series

Playing With Fire

Private Conversation

The Right Groom

After The Fire

Caught In The Flames

Chasing The Fire

Legacy Series

Dark Legacy

Legacy of Lies

Secret Legacy

Emerald City

Investigate Away

Sail Away

The Butterfly Murders

THE AEGIS NETWORK

The Sarich Brother

The Lighthouse

Her Last Hope

The Last Flight

The Return Home

The Matriarch

Aegis Network: Jacksonville Division

A SEAL's Honor

Talon's Honor

Arthur's Honor

Rex's Honor

Kent's Honor

Buddy's Honor

Aegis Network Short Stories

Max & Milian

A Christmas Miracle

Spinning Wheels

Holiday's Vacation

The Brotherhood Protectors

Out of the Wild

Rough Justice

Rough Around The Edges

Rough Ride

Rough Edge

Rough Beauty

The Brotherhood Protectors

The Saving Series

Saving Love

Saving Magnolia

Saving Leather

Hot Hunks

Cove's Blind Date Blows Up

My Everyday Hero – Ledger

Tempting Tavor

Malachi's Mystic Assignment

Needing Neor

Holiday Romances

A Christmas Getaway

Alaskan Christmas

Whispers

Christmas In The Sand

Heroes & Heroines on the Field

Taking A Risk

Tee Time

A New Dawn

The Blind Date

Spring Fling

Summers Gone

Winter Wedding

The Awakening

Fated Moons

The Collective Order

The Lost Sister

The Lost Soldier

The Lost Soul

The Lost Connection

The New Order